What the critics are saying…

"Hill's skill with uncommon characters and very human issues shines in this very different romance." ~ *Ann Leveille from Sensual Romance Reviews*

"*Captive Stallion* is a terrific fantasy novel, filled with love, heroism, sensual delight and heart pounding action." ~ *Enya Adrian from Romance Reviews Today*

"Captive Stallion is something fantasy romance fans should definitely add to their libraries. In fact, it's a book I'd recommend to anyone looking for an emotional erotic romance." ~ *Dani Jacquel Just Erotic Romance Reviews*

"Kate Hill has written another excellent story about these sexy Horsemen. A must read." ~ *Ruby from Fallen Angel Reviews*

KATE HILL

CAPTIVE STALLION

ELLORA'S CAVE
ROMANTICA PUBLISHING

An Ellora's Cave Romantica Publication

www.ellorascave.com

Captive Stallion

ISBN # 1419951998
ALL RIGHTS RESERVED.
Captive Stallion Copyright© 2004 Kate Hill
Edited by: Briana St. James
Cover art by: Syneca

Electronic book Publication: May, 2004
Trade paperback Publication: June, 2005

Warning:

The following material contains graphic sexual content meant for mature readers. *Captive Stallion* has been rated *E-rotic* by a minimum of three independent reviewers.

Ellora's Cave Publishing offers three levels of Romantica™ reading entertainment: S (S-ensuous), E (E-rotic), and X (X-treme).

S-*ensuous* love scenes are explicit and leave nothing to the imagination.

E-*rotic* love scenes are explicit, leave nothing to the imagination, and are high in volume per the overall word count. In addition, some E-rated titles might contain fantasy material that some readers find objectionable, such as bondage, submission, same sex encounters, forced seductions, etc. E-rated titles are the most graphic titles we carry; it is common, for instance, for an author to use words such as "fucking", "cock", "pussy", etc., within their work of literature.

X-*treme* titles differ from E-rated titles only in plot premise and storyline execution. Unlike E-rated titles, stories designated with the letter X tend to contain controversial subject matter not for the faint of heart.

Also by Kate Hill:

Captive Stallion

Horseman

Prologue

The ground shook as hooves pounded across the frost-tipped grass. Powerful equine legs seemed to tangle and sleek coats splashed the field with color as the Horsemen engaged in a polo game. Their wings pressed close to their sides, they galloped after a small wooden ball and struck it with mallets while several onlookers watched from a distance.

Susana drew a deep breath as she stared at the magnificent creatures. In spite of the cold, their well-muscled man torsos and beast bodies glistened with sweat as they laughed and jeered one another. Susana didn't care much for the game. Simply watching the Horsemen was entertainment enough for her. When creating these nearly perfect beings with the heads and torsos of men and a lower half that switched shape from human male to that of a winged horse, the Gods must have been intent on pleasing women. Just looking at Horsemen — particularly a gorgeous one — was enough to drench a woman's pussy and make her soul tingle. To sit astride a Horseman was a fantasy most women shared, yet only a select few were lucky enough to mate with one.

Susana felt lucky. She'd recently struck up a friendship with a handsome young Horseman — an elite Fighting Carrier, nonetheless. Though she'd yet to fly with him, she had ridden him on ground trips. One day, when she overcame her ridiculous fear of heights, she would soar, feeling his mighty legs churn beneath her and his velvet wings beating around her while she pressed close to his broad man-back.

The Horsemen raced past her and she felt the rush of wind as they galloped faster than any true-horse ever could. One of the Horsemen who had been trapped in the midst of the crowd suddenly emerged. His long, sturdy legs seemed to glide over the field as he beat the others to the ball. Susana squirmed a bit, desire tightening her belly at the sight of the lean, hard muscles rippling beneath his rich, brown coat. His corded shoulders and broad, hairy chest flexed as he gripped his mallet. The muscles of his flat, hard-looking abdomen tightened even more as he bent and whacked the ball away from the other Horsemen who had finally reached him. Gods, he was an incredible stallion. He turned and headed back toward the village square, passing her again. His short brown hair was slick with sweat. Rivulets streaked his face and the tanned flesh of his sculpted torso. His beast-coat gleamed like wet velvet in the sunlight. What would it feel like, to be pressed against that hair-roughened chest, to inhale the fresh, wild scent of his flesh and coat? Susana's clit ached with desire. Her pussy flooded with unfulfilled passion. The Horseman glanced at her and smiled. A warm, friendly smile.

"Good morning, Susana." His voice was deep and oh-so-pleasing to the feminine ear. It was a voice that ripped through a woman's veneer of propriety and freed her innermost desires. It rumbled in his chest, yet flowed with the precision and beauty of a scholar. Susana wondered how it would sound close to her ear, his breath tickling her cheek and neck. She shook her head. Ridiculous. Stupid. Yet, why was her heart pounding and her nipples tight and aching beneath her dress?

"Hello, Moor." She forced those horribly lustful thoughts from her head. What was wrong with her? Moor was the last Horseman she should be thinking about. Ever since she'd known him, he'd been a perfect gentleman. Not once had he ever crossed the line of friendship, and that was how it had to be. She wasn't sure what had inspired those odd notions of moments ago. It must have simply been the raw beauty of watching the Horsemen. Most women found them irresistible. Besides, she ought not think about another Horseman when she had Linn all to herself.

Moor's lips parted, as if he was about to speak, but the sound of wings beating overhead drew their attention. They gazed upward. Susana immediately recognized Linn and several other Horsemen flying in for a landing on the village's Running Way.

"Looks like they had a good Gathering," Moor said. "I'll go meet them. See if they need any help unloading cargo."

"Would you tell Linn I'll see him as soon as my rounds are over?"

"Of course. I—"

A sharp cry from the playing field drew their attention. One of the Horsemen—a small, blond-haired buckskin—had fallen to the icy field. Two of the other players paused beside him. Susana hurried to the scene, followed by Moor.

"What happened?" Susana demanded, attempting to stanch the flow of blood from the injured Horseman's leg. Steam from his heated body rose from the icy ground sprayed red with blood.

"One of the sticks broke against my leg."

"Can you get up?" Moor asked.

"I think so."

Moor bent, supporting the injured Horseman as he attempted to stand.

"Careful," Moor said, helping him toward the tack house. Susana's breath caught as she watched the tightening of sculpted muscles in his torso while he helped his companion. Gods, he had a perfect back. It was so broad and covered in smooth skin glowing with sweat. She had the strangest urge to run her hands over it, and down every thick curve of his powerful arms.

What in the world was wrong with her? She had a Horseman of her own, and not only that, she should be concentrating on her patient, not thinking about relationships.

Inside the tack house, she cleaned the man's leg while Moor excused himself to go to the Running Way.

She'd just finished bandaging the Horseman's injury when Moor returned. He strode through the tack house's double doors, passing Susana. The tip of his flowing brown tail brushed her face. Coarse and smooth at the same time, the tail across her skin somehow incited pulsations between her legs and a quickening of her heart that was nothing short of scandalous.

"I'm sorry." Moor glanced at her, his pointed ears twitching and his soul-stealing eyes fixed on her. "How rude of me to stick my tail in your face like that."

"It's no problem." She averted her gaze as she bent to return a bottle of ointment to her bag of healing supplies. Unbelievable. Her hands were actually trembling. Steady hands were one of the attributes the healers she'd learned from had commended her on. Her hands never faltered over the worst of injuries. Now, just from a look of undeniably sensual eyes, they were quivering. In all the years she'd known Moor, she'd held her attraction to him at bay. Suddenly she'd lost all control. Why? What was wrong with her? Now that she had Linn, nothing or no one should affect her in such a way.

"I thought you were going to help at the supply house?" Susana asked.

"When I got there others were already unloading supplies. Too many Horsemen in one supply house causes more harm than good."

"Would you like a grooming, Moor?"

Susana's gaze shot up and fixed on Nellie, a tall, thin, raw-boned woman approaching Moor. Nellie was a groom. A person in her profession could earn a good living, brushing and rubbing down Horsemen. Susana knew the importance of proper care of Horsemen's coat and muscles. She had no problem with legitimate grooms doing honest work, but some had less than admirable reputations. Female grooms, especially, needed to take care when soliciting customers. There were certain women—sluts, really—who called themselves grooms but provided unnecessary "extras" on the side. Though no one in the village talked badly of Nellie, there was something about her that Susana didn't trust. She knew Nellie visited Linn every now and then. The thought of it made her blood heat, but not so much as at this very moment when Nellie lifted a hand toward Moor's equine shoulder, lust gleaming in her pale blue eyes. She stopped just short of touching him.

"May I?" she asked.

He tilted his head to one side, as if thoughtful. Glancing at Susana from the corner of his eye, she thought she detected a hint of — confusion, was it? Annoyance? He looked back at Nellie, smiled slightly, and nodded.

She rested a hand on his rich brown coat. Susana's belly clenched. She knew he felt hot. Horsemen always did, particularly after exercise. Was his coat still damp from the polo game? How sleek and hard his muscles must feel against Nellie's palm. As a healer, Susana had touched many Horsemen. She tried keeping sexual thoughts far from her mind when she treated patients. Remaining professional around such beautiful creatures wasn't always easy, but Susana rarely had a problem with it. Yet when it came to prime specimens such as Linn and Moor, it was especially hard for a woman not to listen to her libido.

"I'm training a new groom to work with me," Nellie continued, her hand sweeping the length of Moor's equine back. She paused at his flank, the expression on her face making the touch far more intimate than necessary. "If you'll let us work on you, I'll only charge you half the usual fee. Grooming a large Horseman will be good practice for her."

"Two grooms for half the price of one?" Moor smiled. "A Horseman would be a fool to say no to that."

"Jane," Nellie bellowed. Susana felt a bit of satisfaction when Moor's sensitive ears flickered at the shrill sound. A younger woman, slim and shorter than Nellie, stepped away from the Horseman she'd been talking to. "Bring the brushes and ointment. We're doing Moor now."

Doing Moor? Susana wasn't sure she appreciated the sound of that.

Moor stepped into a roomy box, about the size of a large stall. Each of the resident Carriers had a box of his own to keep tack, ointment, grooming supplies, and changes of clothes.

The women stepped inside and Susana expected them to close the door. Instead, they left it open. From her position, crouched on the scuffed though clean wooden floor, she saw directly into the box. Nellie stood at Moor's equine rump while Jane positioned herself atop a stool by his man torso.

Susana's mouth went dry as she watched Jane dip a soft cloth into a bowl of warm water and bathe Moor's face and neck. He closed his eyes as the groom-in-training ran the cloth over his shoulders and across the massive expanse of his chest. Rivulets of the clean water trickled down his breastbone and streaked his well-defined abs. Moisture gleamed through the thick mat of hair that tapered down his stomach and flared out in the sleek brown coat covering his equine body.

Crisp air wafted in through the small open window at the back of Moor's box. The breeze reached Susana, carrying the icy outdoor scents, but also Moor's scent. Woodsy, musky, wild and oh-so-delectable. She imagined covering his broad chest with kisses, licking his lean waist, and using her fingertips to trace each and every sculpted abdominal muscle.

At the back of the stall, Nellie used a sweat scraper to clean off his coat, dirty from the polo game. Taking a brush, she stroked it over his rump and across his sturdy back.

Susana had stopped sorting through her bag and stared, her lips parted and her breath quickening as she watched Nellie's palm slide over his well-muscled sides, the brush following her touch. The groom smiled as she slid her fingers over his brown wings. His feathers fluffed a bit. Susana knew they felt as soft as baby chickens but far sleeker. The woman shouldn't be putting her hands on him like that. She had a brush, damn it, and a cloth. Why did she need to stroke his gleaming coat and caress the underside of his belly? When she walked behind him and placed both hands on his rump, Susana's rage hit the boiling point.

"She's a groom, all right," Susana muttered in disgust, jerking the ties tightly on her bag and standing. Heading for the door, she glanced over her shoulder one last time and swallowed hard, resisting the urge to squeeze her thighs together and generate some satisfaction for her throbbing clit and damp pussy. Jane was rubbing ointment into one of Moor's extended arms. The powerful muscles gleamed. His long, elegant fingers moved gracefully as the girl's hands, shiny with ointment, caressed between them and massaged his palms. Nellie had his tail in her hand as she used a comb to unknot the thick brown hair—hair that moments ago had swept across Susana's face in the gentlest, most arousing manner.

Drawing a deep breath, she headed outside. The Running Way and supply house were only a short distance away. Linn was there. Tall, handsome, young Linn who showed such an avid interest in her. What the hell was she doing concerning herself with Moor and his stupid grooms when she had a Fighting Carrier, the best of the best, all to herself?

Susana adjusted her bag of healing supplies more comfortably on her shoulder and headed for the square. Being the only healer in the village kept her busy, but she enjoyed her work. Still, she might have liked more time to spend with Linn. Like Moor, his profession was gathering Rock Blood, a dangerous but necessary task that only the fittest Carriers could attempt. Perhaps with winter coming and the Gathering season soon to be over for the year, they could develop what she hoped to be a lasting relationship. After all, Linn was far more suitable for her than Moor could ever be. Moor was her friend. Linn was her Horseman.

Her brow furrowed. Maybe she hoped for the impossible. Everyone knew each Horseman had the potential to share dreams with his destined mate. The dream sharing struck couples at random and its pull was almost impossible to resist. Linn had never shared dreams with anyone. Yet.

Though some Horsemen married women with whom they'd never shared dreams, there was always the chance that one day the dreams would come. Susana's greatest fear was that she and Linn would fall in love and then his true mate would magically appear.

She told herself to take their relationship slowly. Linn hadn't rushed her, though he'd made his desire plain.

When you're ready, he had told her.

"I am ready," she whispered. "I'm just not exactly *sure*."

Chapter One
Forbidden Desire

Moor narrowed his eyes and lowered his chin against the hail striking his face as he soared over the frozen Spikelands. Even after hours of flying against the wind, the weight of the rider on his back did little to hinder his powerful Horseman physique. His wings beat, the long, sturdy legs of his equine-half churned, and his human torso, covered in a sleek full-coat of hair he could sprout at will, accepted the force of the weather with little distress.

For years Moor had been a Carrier, one of the few Horsemen with the strength and endurance to make the grueling trips to either the frigid north or the scorching tropics to help gather Rock Blood. Without the Rock Blood, humans would die of the plague that swept the world, striking at random and leaving few alive without the cure.

"This weather has been hell tonight," called Jonis, the Gatherer astride Moor's back. Jonis leaned close to Moor's man-torso, trying to absorb some of the tremendous heat generated by the Horseman's body.

"Just remember, things can always get worse," Moor shouted to his partner. For as long as anyone could remember, humans and Horsemen had worked together for the survival of both species. The Horsemen flew Gatherers across seas filled with flesh-eating plants to the only places in the world where Rock Blood existed. In return, human females mated with Horsemen to keep their race alive, since no female Horsemen existed. To many women, mating wasn't simply a bargaining tool. Often, a Horseman would share dreams with a female. When that occurred, the attraction between them was undeniable and often led to the deepest kind of love. Once mated, the Horseman and woman were generally inseparable and parting from one another was nothing short of torture. This was something Moor knew all too well. Years ago, he'd shared dreams with a woman. She'd died, leaving him a young widower, embittered toward an organization he'd once revered.

As the wind picked up, he switched his flight pattern, trying to find a more comfortable level for both him and his rider. While the weather wasn't good, he'd seen worse. In his youth he'd been a Fighting Carrier, elite among his kind. Fighting Carriers not only possessed the greatest speed and endurance of all Horsemen, but they were highly skilled warriors as well. Unlike private Carriers, they dedicated their lives to supporting Rock Blood Gathering while earning little or no profit for themselves. There had been a time when Moor had thought being a Fighting Carrier was the greatest honor a Horseman could aspire to, until they had betrayed him. On the eve of his wife's death, an urgent message had been sent for Moor to return home. The Fighting Carrier in charge of his Gathering Party had kept the message from him until after they'd returned. By the time he reached home, his beloved wife was dead.

Soon after, Moor left the esteemed military organization and became a private Carrier.

"Ready to land?" Moor shouted to his rider as they hovered over one of the smallest northern islands.

"Yes, but I'm not looking forward to the Ice Lizards. This island is loaded with them."

"Just keep your mind on Gathering. Fighting is what we Horsemen do."

Moore signaled to the other Carriers and Gathers. He and a few of the more experienced Carriers led the missions while the others took orders. Since one of the regular Carriers had been injured during an earlier Gathering, Terra, a respected Fighting Carrier as well as the husband of Moor's foster daughter, Inez, had volunteered to fill in on the journey. Like Moor, Terra was permanently stationed in their village of Hornview and was usually the leader of Gatherings. Moor thought highly of the younger man and felt pleased that he and Inez had married.

He thought briefly of Inez as he landed. His last mission as a Fighting Carrier had been to bring Rock Blood to her village that had been hit hard by the plague. He had felt an instant affiliation with the stubborn ten year old girl whose parents had died from the dreaded disease. Together he and Inez had overcome their losses. From an early age, Inez had shown an interest in learning to ride Horsemen. He'd taught her everything she knew. They became partners on journeys. Up until a few months ago when she'd married Terra, they had always attended Gatherings together. Though Moor missed traveling with her, he'd immediately stepped aside when he learned she had a dream lover. In his mind, Inez was his child, and he wanted nothing more than to see her happy. Terra loved her with all his heart, of that he was certain. He knew all too well the magnificence of marrying a dream lover and would do nothing to stand in the way of the gift Inez and the handsome young Fighting Carrier shared.

Moor landed first, his hooves thudding on the island's frozen surface. Gazing skyward, he signaled to the others that it was safe to land. Terra, tall and muscular with a black equine coat, landed next. Several smaller Carriers followed. Kraig, a red-haired Carrier slammed to a landing that sent his rider flying off his back. Moor gritted his teeth. From the moment Kraig had arrived in Hornview, he'd disliked the boy. He was cocky, arrogant, and disrespectful of his riders. His hatred of humans was obvious. Moor wondered why he'd bothered joining the Fighting Carriers whose main purpose was to assist humans through outbreaks of plague. It must have been the prestige of joining the elite group that Kraig desired. Moor didn't doubt that eventually he'd leave the Fighting Carriers and use his skills in private Gatherings where a Horseman could potentially become quite wealthy.

As soon as the Gatherers dismounted, the Horsemen took cloaks and blankets from their saddle packs, draping them over their sweat-drenched bodies to protect them from the severe chill of the Spikelands. The long, grueling flights always raised the temperature of the Horsemen's naturally hot bodies. The shock of bitter cold was almost intolerable for the first few moments after landing.

The Gathering went well until the Ice Lizards attacked. Moor, Terra, and several of the Horsemen posted as guards fought them off. Forming a circle around the Gatherers and the Horsemen assisting in the digging, they battled the thick-skinned, clawed, fanged beasts who dwarfed even the largest of the Carriers.

"There's too many!" bellowed a blond Carrier with a buckskin coat as he used his sword to slash at an Ice Lizard.

"We must have hit a nest," Terra bellowed. The female lizards nested together after mating with the more solitary males. When protecting their unhatched eggs, they fought even more viciously than usual.

The enormous beasts surrounded them. Moor and the other Horsemen used their swords to slash and stab and their equine legs to stomp and kick. The snowy ground turned red with blood, though he was glad to realize it was from the lizards rather than the Horsemen.

Suddenly the blond Carrier's sword was knocked from his hand by one of the lizard's claws. A spiked tail lashed out, sweeping the Carrier's legs from under him. He landed with a grunt on his side. Moor, closest to his fallen comrade, galloped two steps and leapt, his sword slashing the lizard's throat before it could slaughter the other Horseman. Before he landed, a second lizard dropped from an overhanging rock. Moor felt claws slink into his arm and tear before he stabbed his attacker through the heart.

Blood pouring from his arm, Moor continued fighting until weakness drove him to his knees. Terra was beside him in an instant. He and the rest of the party chased off the remainder of the lizards.

Tearing off a section of his blanket, Terra bound Moor's arm to stop the blood flow. The other Horsemen stayed close by to protect them, should the lizards regroup for another attack.

"Are you all right?" Moor's rider, Jonis, approached, concern in his eyes.

Moor nodded. "I just need a few minutes to rest and I'll be fine."

"I won't take any cargo with us," Jonis said.

"No, with the plague outbreaks, the towns have been desperate for Rock Blood. I can carry."

"Make it light," Terra told Jonis who nodded.

After a few moments, Moor's head cleared and he got to his feet. Jonis filled his saddle packs only halfway before mounting. Normally such a light load would have been nothing to Moor. A Carrier of his size and condition had no problem supporting the weight of the saddle, fifty to seventy-five pounds of cargo and a hundred forty pound rider for long journeys. Tonight, however, Moor was grateful that Jonis was skinny as a child and the load light. Still, he felt confident that he could make the flight home, even injured. He had to. The Spikelands were too dangerous for anyone to remain for more than a couple of hours. Unfortunately, once out of the islands, there would be no place to rest until they reached home. Hundreds of miles of oceans filled with the killer plants stretched between the Spikelands and Hornview that stood on the northern-most coast of the civilized world.

"You're sure you're feeling all right?" Jonis asked before he and Moor galloped for takeoff.

"Don't worry, I won't drop you," Moor told him. "If we go down, it will be together."

"Oh, that's reassuring."

"I have no intention of dying in the Spikelands or in the sea."

"Just hold that thought, will you, my friend?" Jonis tried to sound teasing, but his worry was apparent in the uneasy way he sat in the saddle.

In truth, Moor felt much better than he expected. Perhaps the excitement of the fight had provided him with extra energy. Often, when Horsemen were tested, some hidden reserve kicked in, pushing them past their already tremendous capacity of strength and endurance.

Moor had never dropped or harmed a rider in his life, even during the worst of journeys.

The flight went better than expected until the last of the Spikelands faded in the distance, leaving only the endless stretch of sea. A sharp turn to keep himself righted against a powerful gust of wind drew fresh blood flow from Moor's injured arm. He gasped with pain and squeezed his free hand to the arm. Jonis tore off part of a blanket in the saddle pack and helped Moor bind the injury again—a difficult procedure while in midair. Moments later, he'd bled through the bandage. Moor felt light-headed from blood loss. Sweat soaked his coat. His lungs felt ready to explode from gasping in the frigid air.

Gods, it's too far to go. His heart pounded, skipping beats as he struggled to keep himself on an even flight pattern.

"I'm unloading the cargo," Jonis called to him.

Unable to expend the energy to reply, Moor continued flying. Through blurry eyes, he thought he saw the water looming close, the dark, deadly reeds stretching toward his churning equine legs.

"Pull up. Pull up," Jonis bellowed. "We're too close to the ocean!"

Moor did his best to fly upward against the wind. His breath rasped and he felt Jonis press closer to his man-torso as he struggled to unfasten the saddle. They'd risked their lives to gather the Rock Blood humans desperately needed and the saddle was one of his best, but at that moment Moor didn't care about either. Survival was foremost in his mind. Survival and agony. His lungs and muscles were on fire and the loss of blood had weakened him so much he felt on the verge of blacking out. Suddenly the weight of the saddle was gone and he managed a deep breath. He forced his wings and legs upward. Was he succeeding in his ascent?

"Moor," a voice bellowed to his left.

He forced himself to focus on Terra. Another Horseman dropped near his right, holding a support strap.

Terra loomed close, his rider reaching for Jonis. Was the younger Horseman crazy? How could he possibly fly the rest of the way home with two riders and cargo? Such a flight could kill a Carrier. Still, Terra was powerful and well-trained. He might be able to handle it. Moor himself had undergone flights with unusually heavy loads. Just by taking his rider, Terra was probably saving his life as well as Jonis's. Moor knew he had the strength to fly for himself, though he would have sank to his death before ever unloading a rider.

With the burden of his rider gone, Moor's head cleared and his breathing became easier. He felt something graze his belly. The Horseman to his left had thrown the support line underneath Moor's equine body and another Carrier caught it from the other side. The two smaller Horsemen rose over his head. One of them held both ends of the strap. If Moor felt the need, he could lean on the strap to rest during the flight home while the Carrier above helped support him.

Knowing he had assistance, that the others in his party were willing to risk their lives to help him and Jonis, fueled his strength. He beat his wings harder and after a moment rose to a safe distance above the sea.

Not once did he lean into the support strap, unwilling to overburden the Carrier above him unless absolutely forced to. Several times the other members of the party flew in to offer help. Only one Carrier refused to assist. Kraig flew ahead, only glancing back to fire looks of rage and jealousy at Terra who flew just ahead of Moor, his motions remarkably steady for a Horseman carrying too much weight. As the journey progressed, Moor noted through his own discomfort, that Terra flew more slowly than usual. The wind blew lather from his black equine coat, revealing the toll taken on his overburdened body. Moor felt overwhelmed with gratitude for his friend and rage toward Kraig. The redhead was also a large Carrier, well able to share the burden of the second rider for at least part of the journey. Terra was a true Fighting Carrier, but Moor wondered how Kraig had even earned a position in the elite force. It took more than speed and power to be a Fighting Carrier. It took loyalty, courage, and heart, qualities that Kraig didn't have.

By the end of the journey, Moor had lost so much blood he was almost unconscious in flight. His wings beat and legs churned without thought. As torch lights from the Running Way near the village square shone like fuzzy dots in the distance, Moor wondered if the vision of home wasn't some trick of his dying mind.

His crash landing proved that he was still very much alive. His knees scraped the packed dirt ground and his equine body slammed hard on its side. What wind he had left was knocked out of him. Unable to do more than gasp and wheeze, he lay still until he felt gentle arms slip around him. Tender, frantic hands probed his bloodied torso. As his eyes focused on Inez, he felt awash with relief. His foster daughter looked terrified as she searched for his wound.

"Arm," he grunted in pain.

Suddenly another pair of small hands found the wound. These hands were sure and deft as they sliced away the bloodied piece of blanket and began cleansing the injury.

His eyes focused on Susana. Though young, she was highly skilled. Blonde hair fell across her delicate face as she worked on his arm. He thought she said something about cauterizing the wound, but he was nearly unconscious again. The burning of his flesh roused him slightly and he groaned.

Inez asked what happened to Moor's rider. Someone told her Terra had flown him in. Moments later, she was gone, probably to see to her husband. In the back of his mind, Moor hoped Terra hadn't damaged himself by making such an arduous flight carrying two men and cargo.

"You'll be all right," Susana told him in a soothing voice. Her hand gently gripped his shoulder. "Linn and a few others have gone for some buckets of water to cool you down, then you can get back to the longhouse and rest."

Water. Thank the Gods. His body felt hot enough to explode. Suddenly he was doused with several buckets of cool water. Slowly, his body temperature returned to normal. With the bleeding finally stopped, he felt able to stand.

Linn, a sturdy buckskin Fighting Carrier, helped him to his feet. The rugged, blond-haired youth was courting Susana. The talk of the village was that the two might someday marry. Moor thought they made a fine-looking couple, the pretty little pale-haired healer and the powerful blond Horseman. Both were young and had their whole lives ahead of them. What he wouldn't give to feel love and companionship again, though part of him was glad he never would. Losing his wife had been too painful. Still, he wouldn't have traded a moment spent with her. Since her death, he hadn't considered another serious relationship. Oh, he released sexual tension with some very willing women who preferred the shapeshifting Horsemen to human males. When Horsemen focused on their Turning Point located in their lower man-back, they were able to shift from half-horse to a full man-body, called Huform, enabling them to mate with women. In general, Horsemen were very tall, hard-muscled, and extremely well endowed. In Huform, their cocks and balls rivaled those of true-horses, but their endurance far surpassed the weaker species in every way. Nature had blessed Horsemen, and women had been born to enjoy them.

Moor's legs trembled as he dragged himself to the longhouse a short distance from the running way. Though owned by Hornview's Chieftain, the longhouse was always open to the villagers. Susana's herbarium was there, and she cared for most of her patients in her own private room in the back of it.

Linn remained by Moor's side, supporting him, until he collapsed by the enormous fireplace taking up most of one wall in the longhouse.

Though weak, he concentrated on his Turning Point, shuddering as he changed to Huform, so lying down indoors would be easier. Someone pulled a blanket over his naked body and placed a soft pillow under his head.

His eyes opened halfway, fixing on Susana. She smiled and brushed damp hair from his eyes. He knew she was only doing her duty, but she was the sort of healer who made everyone feel important. She never treated anyone with the callousness some healers developed.

"I'll bring you some water and something to eat," she said. Long eyelashes cast shadows across her full, golden-skinned cheeks. A light spray of freckles across her snubbed nose made her appear even younger. It seemed impossible such a little girl was one of the finest healers in the north.

"Thank you for what you've done," he said.

Susana smiled gently. "It's my job. Besides, I'm not going to let anything bad happen to you after all the years we've known each other."

Since he and Inez had moved to the village over seven years ago, Susana had been a good friend to both. Moor was glad, since Inez spent so much time with Carriers that she rarely associated with other women. Susana, also consumed with her work, had been a kindred spirit to his foster daughter. How many times had he shared meals with both young women and acted as a mediator during their occasional arguments?

No sooner had Susana left than Moor drifted to sleep, thoroughly exhausted from his injury and the difficult journey.

* * * * *

In the darkness of the longhouse, Moor discerned the delicate silhouette seated close to him on the floor. The fire burned low, yet when the figure turned, a ray of moonlight glowing through a distant window revealed Susana's pert features.

"How are you feeling?" she asked.

"Better." Moor realized his injury scarcely hurt at all. This had to be a dream, yet it was so clear, so real. The only dreams that could be like this were shared dreams, and it was impossible that he and Susana were sharing one. He sat up straighter, his gaze fixed on the young healer. Gods, why had he never realized her expression was intoxicating? Her eyes, deep blue and almost too large for her face, were beautiful, but he'd always admired them as one would appreciate a sculpture or a sunset. Those eyes suddenly appeared earthy and passionate as she edged closer, her small hands reaching for his injured arm. She inspected the bandage.

Moor's pulse quickened. Beneath the blanket covering his lap, his cock swelled. What the hell was wrong with him? This girl was too young for him. She was his foster daughter's best friend, and she had already been claimed by another Horseman, one far more suitable for her.

His large hand covered both of hers and gently removed them from his arm. "I'm fine."

Susana's lips parted slightly as she smiled, leaning closer. "Yes," she whispered against his mouth, "you are fine."

Her full, soft lips covered his. Moor knew he should stop her, but his soul caught fire. Her blonde hair tickled his face as her lips moved against his. Moor grasped her upper arms and tugged her closer. Parting her lips with his tongue, he explored her warm, wet mouth. Susana sighed, a soft sound of desire. Her hands slipped over his shoulders and grasped his back, her fingers, slim yet strong, clutching his powerful muscles.

Moor's heart thrummed as if he'd just flown to the Spikelands and back. His chest rose and fell with each anxious breath. The sensation of her firm, full breasts pressing close to his body turned his cock to steel.

He grasped her shoulders and tugged her away, holding her at arms' length. His need for her was driving him to madness. It was a physical ache deep inside him, spurred by the herbal scent of her skin and the echo of her excited breathing in the stillness around them. Her glistening, kiss-bruised lips were almost too tempting to resist, but he had to.

"What the hell are we doing?" he demanded in a harsh whisper.

She appeared as bewildered as he felt. "I don't know. I can't seem to help myself. I feel if I don't make love with you I'll go mad."

"Not before I do." He shoved her away, not hard enough to hurt her, but hopefully enough to discourage any further displays of passion.

Susana stared at him, her lips parted as if to speak. Tears glittered in her eyes before she fled across the longhouse and disappeared in the darkness.

* * * * *

Moor snapped awake, his heart slamming against his chest and his injured arm aching. He'd thrown off his blanket and his pillow lay halfway across the room.

"Gods." He pushed himself to his knees, breathless. His gaze swept the room for any sign of Susana. He could still taste her, feel her. Her scent encompassed him. Trying to ignore his swollen, aching cock, he stood and headed for the door. There was no way he could stay at the longhouse for the remainder of the night, not when it would mean seeing her again.

Though he still felt a little weak from his injury, the rest had rejuvenated him a bit and changing shape had helped speed the healing process within his body. He knew he could manage the short walk to his cottage on the outskirts of the village. In his own home, he might be able to better control his crazy desires for Susana.

Wrapping the blanket around his waist, he left the house and crossed the village square on bare human feet. Why couldn't he stop feeling her delicate little hands on his back? Why couldn't he expel the sweet taste of her lips? The last time he'd experienced such a potent dream had been years ago when he'd shared dreams with his wife. Those hadn't been normal dreams, but genuine experiences involving a man and woman joined by the magic that introduced some lucky Horsemen to their destined mates.

"No," Moor murmured as he quickened his pace. He dropped the blanket and shuddered, the ground beneath him shaking as he switched to his equine-half. Ignoring the moment of weakness following the change, he broke into a canter, scarcely missing a beat. "It can't be. Not again. It's impossible."

His speed increased until his hooves scarcely touched the ground. He spread his wings for takeoff but before he ascended, weakness washed over him and the world momentarily turned black. Slowing, he caught himself as he stumbled and nearly struck the ground. He stood, panting, his injured arm throbbing, and gazed at the moon high in the clear midnight sky.

It was unheard of for a Horseman to share dreams with more than one woman in a lifetime. Whatever had happened back in the longhouse was *not* a magical dream. It must have been some trick of the mind after enduring the flight from the Spikelands while nearly bleeding to death. That was all. He'd probably never dream of Susana again.

His pulse slowing, he turned and walked home. After a good night's sleep in his own bed, everything would be right again. He wouldn't have enough strength to make the final journey to the Spikelands tomorrow, before the Gathering stopped for the winter season, so he might as well leave early to visit his brother and his family a few villages away. Usually he and Inez visited them together, but this winter she had her new husband. They would enjoy their time alone. It would be good for them.

Pushing open his front door, Moor paused in the center of the single, spacious room and switched back to Huform. He didn't bother lighting a fire since his Horseman body usually generated enough heat to keep him warm even in cold weather. Moor was taller and more muscular than most other Carriers. He'd been the biggest in the village until Terra arrived. In his youth, many had thought him too thickly-muscled to be a good, fast, endurance flyer, but he'd proven his critics wrong. In his short time with the Fighting Carriers, he'd earned many honors. Of course he'd broken a rule or two along the way, he remembered with a grin, and nearly broken himself as well, but no one had ever dared insinuate again he couldn't travel fast over long distances.

As he sprawled, stomach-down, on his bed, pulling a sheet over his buttocks, he closed his eyes and drifted. Half-asleep, he shrugged his broad shoulders, yet he was unable to brush away the sensation of Susana's lovely hands on his back.

* * * * *

Susana awoke, her body tingling, though an unsettled feeling weighted her breast.

What a strange dream. She'd been in Moor's arms.

Perhaps it's not so strange after all.. She slipped on her robe and belted it. First those lustful thoughts while watching him play in the field, now this dream that left her heart pounding and pussy drenched.

Moor might be her best friend's foster father, but he was no sway-backed old Horseman ready to be put out to pasture. Though Moor had raised Inez since she was ten, he'd been only a youth himself when he'd found her, orphaned. He was only eight years Susana's senior, and while she'd hidden her desire, she'd always considered him one of the handsomest Horsemen ever. His body, both in human and half-beast form, was exquisite. Though rugged, his features were well-formed. His large amber eyes seemed to reach into a woman's soul. Yet his good looks were only part of his attraction. Moor was sincere.

Everything he did was with a pure heart that was willing to expend itself for those he held dear. If he hadn't raised Inez and if he hadn't once shared dreams with a woman he still loved, Susana might have approached him for something more than friendship. Of course that was before she met Linn. She and Linn were falling in love and she surely didn't want to ruin the real relationship she could have with him for some silly fantasy about a Horseman who had never been anything more than a good friend.

Susana left her room in the longhouse and entered the main hall. Perhaps she should check on Moor. He'd nearly died earlier. Maybe that incited her dream about him. She'd always been able to ignore her attraction, but he'd never required her skills before. Though she was a healer, trained to remain impartial to those in her care, seeing him vulnerable had done something to her. She'd wanted to soothe him, make his pain disappear, see him powerful again.

The fire had burned down, dimming the entire hall, yet as she approached the hearth, she realized Moor was gone.

"Moor?" she called softly in the darkness, glancing around. She peered into an alcove and lifted her chin to the loft. Other than several sleeping servants, the hall was empty.

She hurried to where Linn slept. Since he had only been sent to Hornview as a temporary Fighting Carrier, Linn stayed in the longhouse rather than building a home of his own. Susana gazed at the sleeping Horseman and thought how handsome he was. In Huform, Linn sprawled on his back, wearing only loose trousers. Like Moor and Terra, he was large for a Carrier, his young body well-muscled. His blond hair was in disarray, half concealing his smooth features.

"Linn." Susana knelt and shook him gently.

He leapt awake, his long, pointed Horseman ears wiggling as his senses came alive. "What's wrong?"

"Moor's gone."

"Gone?" Linn's brow furrowed.

"He's not by the fire. I'm going to look for him. Will you come?"

"Of course." Linn stood, running a hand across his sleepy eyes and rubbing his chin.

"I hope he's all right."

"I'm sure he's fine. You know how fast our kind heal. He probably got sick of sleeping on the floor by the fire and decided to go home."

"I hope so. He lost so much blood tonight that he might not be as strong as he thinks."

"Don't worry." Linn squeezed her hand as they left the longhouse. Her insides warmed. Linn really was sweet.

Outside, she respectfully glanced away as he removed his trousers and switched from Huform. The ground trembled and she knew it was done. When she turned back, Linn stood still on four long legs, his eyes closed as he waited through the few seconds of weakness that always followed shapeshifting. She glanced over his equine form, admiring the powerful muscles rippling beneath his smooth buckskin coat, his tan wings pressed close to his sides.

His eyes opened and he approached the fence by the longhouse so Susana could step on it to mount. Her heart fluttered as she did so. Before Linn, she'd never ridden a Horseman. She still wouldn't fly with him. He told her not to worry. Someday she'd be ready. For now, he just kept their trips to easy canters across the meadows.

Arriving at Moor's cottage, they peered in the window.

"See. I told you he's fine," Linn said.

Susana swallowed and drew a deep breath. Inside, Moor lay, naked, stomach down on the bed, the taut globes of his buttocks exposed. A blanket, most likely tossed off in sleep, lay on the floor beside the bed. The muscles of his broad shoulders and back stood out, well-defined, even while relaxed in sleep. Dark hair dusted his long hard-looking thighs and calves. She shivered.

"Cold?" Linn asked. "You must be freezing. That robe isn't nearly warm enough for a human in this weather. I'm getting you back to the longhouse."

"Thanks, Linn. I'm sorry to wake you up."

"That's never a problem. Like you said, he lost plenty of blood. He might have been hurt somewhere."

Susana's fingers tightened affectionately on Linn's strong shoulders.

"How about cuddling by the fire for the rest of the night?" He grinned at her, his tone humorous, though his eyes held an open invitation.

Their relationship had grown even closer of late, yet they had never kissed and only occasionally embraced. His offer was definitely a step toward romance. Perhaps it was about time she took the risk. Immersing herself in a gorgeous young stallion such as Linn would be enough to curb any ridiculous—and impossible—feelings she had regarding Moor.

"Sounds wonderful," she said.

His ears pricked upward. "Really?"

"Yes." She ruffled his sandy blond hair as he approached the longhouse.

In moments, they were doing just as he suggested. Linn had rekindled the fire while Susana brought over pillows and a blanket. Lying on her side, she snuggled close to Linn who slipped his arms around her, holding her to his chest. Linn was a wonderful young man and they cared for each other. What more could she ask for?

Closing her eyes, she sighed. In those final moments between wakefulness and sleep, she caught another scent and felt another body enfolding hers.

Gods. What was she going to do if her restrained attraction for Moor suddenly became obsession?

Chapter Two
Forbidden

The following morning, though all his strength hadn't returned from his ordeal, Moor felt better. Guilt over his lack of participation in the year's final Gathering nagged him a bit.

When he arrived at the village square, neither Terra nor Inez were at the Running Way. He wasn't surprised. After last night, he was sure Terra felt muscles he never realized he possessed. Considering he still had one more flight to make that afternoon, he was smart to rest while he could.

"Hello."

Moor spun at the sound of Susana's voice. Memories of his dream flooded him and his heart pounded.

"How are you feeling?" She approached, reaching for his bandaged arm.

"Much better. Almost good enough to go on this afternoon's flight. In fact—"

"Absolutely not." Her gaze flew to his. He thought she blushed, but before he could be certain, she lowered her head to study his arm and her hair fell across her face. "There's no way you can handle that, Moor. You might feel good now, but halfway to the Spikelands you'll probably start sinking again. Give yourself at least a few more days before any hard traveling."

He sighed. She was probably right. He wasn't ready for another long journey yet. His next thought floated off when the bandage fell away and her soft hands examined his bare flesh. Damn, why couldn't he focus when he was around her? He'd known her for years. By the way she was acting, she had not shared his dream last night. She was too matter-of-fact, too in control.

"You're healing very well," she said. "Come to the longhouse and I'll get you a fresh bandage."

He followed her, wondering how he would endure the winter in the village with no Gatherings to go on and Susana so close by. An idea struck him.

"Since the winter season's here and there won't be any flights to the North until spring, I think I'll visit my brother in Gullville. I feel well enough to leave tonight, unless you think I'm in any grave danger?" A smile played around his lips.

"I don't see what harm that could do, as long as you take it slow. Do you really want to leave tonight? Why not wait a few days?"

Moor's eyes followed the gentle swish of her shapely backside as she led him through the longhouse to her room at the end of the hall.

"Because I need the time away," he said as they stepped inside.

"I can understand that. I've often felt that way myself." She motioned toward one of the chairs around the small wooden table by the fireplace. He sat as she brought salve and bandages.

As she worked, they remained silent. He was glad she kept her eyes focused on his arm because he couldn't seem to stop staring at her. The spray of freckles across her nose was so adorable. Her full lips looked so kissable.

Stop. You cannot have her.

"There." She sat back, her gaze fixed on his, her lips parted. "Moor, I'm so glad you're feeling better."

"I owe my recovery to you as much as to Terra. Thank you."

"I was doing my job."

"And you do it well."

She smiled. "I have to get started on my rounds then Linn and I are going to the lake for a meal."

The mention of the younger man spending time with her made the hair on the back of his neck bristle.

Her brow furrowed. "Is something wrong?"

"No, why?"

"You just looked angry for a minute. Your ears are pinned."

"They are?" Moor hadn't even realized. He wiggled them and forced a smile. "I was just thinking about last night. Such accidents annoy me."

"Just annoy?" She shook her head, her eyes glistening with amusement. "You Carriers are a rugged lot."

He followed her out of the longhouse where they parted, her heading toward the village square while he turned back toward the tack house near the Running Way. He turned, glancing at her over his shoulder and was stunned that she was staring at him as well. A surprised look flashed between them and both turned away quickly. Moor's pace quickened along with his pulse. No, he couldn't get out of Hornview fast enough. A trip to his brother's village was exactly what he needed to get over this foolish obsession.

* * * * *

Moor waited until Terra and Inez returned from the Gathering that night before leaving for his brother's village. He'd almost reconsidered his trip until Susana had come to the Running Way to meet Linn. The way she'd stared at the young Horseman, his lean muscles taut from the long journey, had been almost too much for Moor to stand. He'd kissed Inez goodbye, shook hands with Terra, and left right away.

As he flew through the starlit sky, he began feeling a little better. Now that Susana was miles away, he could stop acting like a lovesick colt and get back to normal. It seemed like forever since he'd seen his brother's family. When Inez was still a child, they'd visit every year. Even after she reached adulthood, they'd traveled there together. It would be strange visiting without her, but he knew she and Terra would enjoy having so much time together over the winter season. Maybe they'd have a child. It would be so nice, watching Inez's daughter or son grow up.

The night was pleasantly warm for winter and Moor felt so much better that he picked up speed. He loved flying and it was difficult to restrain himself, though Susana's warning resounded in his mind. Susana. He had to stop thinking of her.

Remember Anita, the woman who truly shared *your* dreams. Anita would always have a piece of Moor's heart. They'd been so young when they started sharing dreams. When they'd married, they were only fifteen years old. Moor had been very tall and big for his age. It must have been the Highlander blood on his mother's side. No other Horsemen had Highlanders' power. They could pull loads that would knock Fighting Carriers off their feet. While Moor was not as strong as a traditional Highlander, that blood in his veins had served him well when carrying a rider and heavy cargo to and from the Spikelands. As a youth, the only thing he'd wanted as much as Anita was to become a Fighting Carrier. Due to his body structure, he'd been told he couldn't make it as a Fighting Carrier, since most were proportioned differently than Moor. Still, he'd passed the test for the Fighting Carriers and surprised those who had called him a failure before he'd begun. Not only was his speed well above average, but even experienced Fighting Carriers fell short of his endurance record. At sixteen, he'd been initiated into the esteemed military organization. For two years he flew missions in the Spikelands as well as in the tropics and garnered a reputation as a Horseman who could fly through anything. He'd been proud of his career and it pleased him that Anita seemed happy with him as well. The young couple spent every moment of his leave time together. They'd been planning a trip to Gray Flats when she died.

Moor's chest tightened with the memory. His wings pounded air as he unconsciously increased his speed as he remembered another flight from long ago.

Moor recalled flying home as fast as possible, not even bothering to rest after the arduous Gathering he'd just completed. Anita's body lay cold in their bed. He'd held her, kissed her, but it wasn't the same. There was no warmth or softness in that corpse. Anita was gone and he hadn't been able to say goodbye.

"No," Moor whispered. Tears stung his eyes and not just from the speed of his flight. "I can't do it again. Not with another woman. Once was enough."

Even if by the slim chance he and Susana were sharing dreams, he couldn't succumb to the magical lure.

His pulse skipped as he slowed his pace. Below, firelight shone in the window of his brother's farmhouse. Suddenly he realized he hadn't sent a message about his coming. He shouldn't just drop in. Thoughts of Susana had clouded all others.

He was about to turn toward the nearest village and take a room at the inn when he heard wings beating nearby.

"Moor. Hey." His brother, a tall, burly Horseman, shouted as he flew closer. Like Moor, Pete had brown hair and a rich brown coat, but his two rear legs had white socks and streaks of white colored his dark tail.

"I meant to send a message that I wanted to visit. I was just on my way to the village to get a room—"

"Nonsense. Lina and I will be damn mad if you don't stay with us. Your nephew has been asking about you for months."

"How is Silas?"

"Growing like a weed, as they say. He's going to be a good-sized Horseman, considering he has Highland blood on our side as well as on Lina's. He's been talking about becoming a puller when he grows up."

Moor grinned. "A puller, huh? Good ones can make plenty of money at the fairs, but it's a rough job."

"That's what I told him. He's got time to think, though. He's only twelve years old. Why don't we land and cool down? Lina probably has supper ready."

"Are you sure I'm not imposing?"

"Not at all. Let's go."

Together, the brothers descended. The impact of the ground beneath Moor's hooves felt good. Susana was right. Even after the fairly short flight, he felt a little tired. He hadn't traveled too quickly, though, and only felt a little hot.

"What happened?" Pete nodded at Moor's bandaged arm.

He briefly recounted the Gathering. When he finished, Pete looked grave.

"It's a risky business you're in, Moor. Your friend Terra sounds like a great Horseman. He and Inez get along well?"

"They were made for each other."

"That's nice to hear. I felt that way about Lina. When I saw her, I said to myself, that's one hell of a woman. And when I found out her father was one of us, I knew we were meant to be."

"You two have made a nice life for yourselves."

"Other than the accident, how have you been?"

"Fine."

As they neared the farmhouse, the door flew open and a tall, lanky boy raced toward them on four swift equine legs. "Uncle Moor. I didn't know you were coming."

"Hi, Silas." Moor grinned. "You've gotten tall, boy."

"Look at this." Silas balled his fist, revealing a respectable muscle in his arm. "I've been pulling the sledge for months. Pretty soon I'll be pulling as much as Dad."

Pete raised an eyebrow and ruffled Silas's hair. "You've got a while to go for that, but I don't doubt that by the time you're grown you'll be pulling even more than me."

"You should have seen the pulling contest at the fair this past summer, Uncle Moor. Someday, that's what I'm going to do."

"We need to cool down, so why don't you walk with us and tell me all about it?" Moor said.

"Uncle Moor, remember that big Highlander Frederic who beat you in the pulling contest at the fair last year?"

"Oh, yes." Moor grinned. "My back wouldn't let me forget him."

"He pulled the biggest load I ever saw."

"I don't doubt it," Moor said as they headed for the meadow behind the house.

* * * * *

"What are you thinking about?" Linn asked.

Susana blinked and shifted her position on Linn's equine back. "I'm sorry, did you say something?"

"Your mind has been wandering for the past week."

Susana couldn't deny his accusation. Lately her work was all that kept her thoughts off Moor. Since he'd gone, her obsession with him had increased. Memories of that strange dream about him nagged her. It had felt so real that she wondered if truly being in his arms would be as wonderful as the fantasy.

She scolded herself. Why would she think of any other man when she had the pleasure of Linn's company? She concentrated on feeling the play of his hard, young muscles as he strode toward the longhouse in the village square. His silky tail brushed his hindquarters and her back with gentle, sweeping motions.

"I shouldn't complain," he said. "Being a healer, you must have so much on your mind."

"I'm sorry," she repeated. "I don't know what's been wrong with me lately."

She dismounted in front of the longhouse and stepped in front of Linn, gazing up at him. Bending, he kissed her cheek. They exchanged a warm embrace.

"I have to get to the tack house and prepare for the next Gathering, so I probably won't see you until tomorrow."

"Maybe we can take another walk to the lake? It's so pretty when it's frozen."

"Sounds fine." He stroked her cheek with the back of his hand. "Have you thought more about flying?"

Susana's belly tightened with fear at the idea of soaring so high above the ground. "I don't think I'm ready yet."

He smiled slightly, hiding disappointment well. "All right. Bye, Susana."

"Have a good flight, Linn. Be safe."

"I will." He grinned at her over his shoulder. She watched until he disappeared in the tack house before fetching her bag from her room and making her rounds of the village.

The day proved so busy for Susana that she was able to forget about both Moor and Linn as she concentrated on delivering twins for the blacksmith's wife and helping two men who were injured in a wagon wreck.

Late that night, she finally crawled into bed, exhausted, and fell asleep instantly.

* * * * *

A gentle fingertip traced Susana's lips. Her eyelids lifted and she found herself gazing at Moor.

Gods, another dream.

His fingertips moved to her jaw then stroked hair from her forehead. Her gaze swept the broad, hair-roughened chest so close she only had to reach out to feel the beating of his heart. As if unable to stop herself, she did just that, sitting up slightly and placing her palm on the hard plate of muscle. Like all Horsemen, his flesh felt incredibly warm. Her fingers tightened, sinking deeper into the mat of soft brown hair.

"Moor?" she murmured, not wishing to destroy the mood yet needing some form of verbal communication.

Her hand fell away from his chest as he paused in stroking her face. It was then she realized he was completely naked. Her gaze fixed on the gorgeous cock that swelled in its nest of dark brown hair, the balls beneath heavy and perfectly formed.

What the hell was wrong with her? She was a healer, accustomed to the bodies of humans and Horsemen. But she was also a woman. At that moment she had never felt more feminine in her entire life.

Her hand curved around his hard shoulder muscle. Suddenly he grasped her upper arms and dragged her onto his lap, groaning as he kissed her forehead and temples. Susana clung to him. His mouth covered hers in a kiss so hot and penetrating that she lost all thought and became a creature of pure sensation. His tongue stroked hers while his hands slid up her bare back. Susana didn't question her nakedness but locked her legs around his waist. His steely cock pressed against her aching clit. Her pussy felt so hot, wet, and ready to be filled with his muscle and flesh. She rocked against him, her hands gripping his broad back, enjoying the sensation of his hairy chest scraping her nipples.

Raising herself slightly, she curled her fist around his cock, loving the sensation of velvet skin over steely hardness. She guided him inside her slick pussy, marveling at how perfectly he filled her.

Moor buried his face in her neck. Wrapping her arms around him, she held him tightly, nuzzling his short brown hair.

"Gods, this is wrong," he breathed.

Susana shook her head and tightened her grip. "I know, but I don't care. I need this, Moor. I need you."

He groaned, a deep rumble in his broad chest. Desire stabbed her core. As she rocked harder against him, Moor grasped her buttocks and helped her move. His hands felt so warm and strong, the palms callused, his grip firm yet never painful.

"Moor, oh," she cried, gripping him so tightly she doubted a human male could have drawn a breath. Even in Huform, Horsemen were so much more powerful than normal men and Moor was stronger than an average Carrier. Susana reveled in the sensation of his granite muscles and scarcely restrained energy. She felt wrapped in hot skin, solid muscle, and his marvelous outdoorsy scent. His teeth and tongue played with her earlobe, his breath warm against her face. Suddenly she convulsed, her entire body pulsing in the best orgasm of her life.

As she gasped, his hands clasped her face and his mouth covered hers, absorbing her rapturous cries. As the last wave of pleasure ebbed, Moor pressed her onto the mattress and loomed above her.

She stared deeply into his eyes, feeling another orgasm building, inspired by his expression of perfect desire. His amber eyes seemed to glow as he gently spread her legs and knelt between them, kissing her inner thighs. His tongue stroked her clit, exploring the passion-plumped flesh. Susana closed her eyes, her head arching into the pillow, her fingers sifting through his hair and feeling the smooth, bare flesh of his nape.

He slid up her body and entered her with a long, slow thrust. Susana wrapped her arms and legs around him, her hips mimicking his motions. Gods, he felt so good. His body temperature was so hot, his strength so overpowering. He could have hurt her with his big, hard-muscled body, yet all she felt was pleasure.

"Susana," he murmured before covering her mouth with his.

His tongue explored every warm, moist inch of her mouth then fought a sensual duel with hers until he tore his head away. Gasping, he plunged into her fast and hard, driving her toward another perfect orgasm. She cried out, her body throbbing. As her pussy clenched his rock-hard erection, his hips jerked in several fast thrusts that hurled him into bliss.

He melted onto her, his big body covering hers, his lips buried in the curve of her neck.

"We shouldn't have—" he began.

"I know," she interrupted, feeling a bit sick inside. They couldn't continue like this. She knew the more they gave in to their dreams, the harder it would be to keep away from one another in the real world.

* * * * *

Moor snapped awake, drenched in sweat, his heart pounding. A tremendous erection throbbed between his legs.

"Damn it," he hissed, standing from his cot. He left the cottage, careful not to awaken Pete, Lina, and Silas who slumbered, lost in a peaceful sleep he envied.

He'd hoped the dream about Susana had been a fluke. Now his worst fear weighed like steel on his heart. Though he didn't want to admit it, part of him knew the dreams were magical.

Why Susana? Why after so many years?

An old legend stated that the dreams would fade if both parties denied them. He and Susana had relished the fantasy tonight, but both had made it clear a relationship between them could never be.

Perhaps if he immersed himself in something else he could forget about her and the dreams would fade. Maybe he could fly to the tropics and join Gathering Parties there until winter. Of course his regular Gatherer wouldn't accompany him. Jonis always spent the off-season with his family. Still, Moor knew he would have no problem finding a temporary rider.

He shook his head as he stepped outside, removing his trousers and freeing his cock to the chilly night air. No, more Gatherings weren't what he needed. Of course they would keep him occupied during the journeys, but he required something that would fill his every waking moment, something that would obsess him as much as thoughts of the pretty young healer.

Suddenly, an idea struck him.

Closing his eyes, he concentrated on his Turning Point. He shuddered as his human half molded and expanded, leaving him with his sturdy equine-half. He broke into a gallop, his hooves flying across the frost-covered meadow before he took to the air. His wings beat as he flew, heading toward Kingsville, fifty miles south. Each year the village hosted an endurance race called The King Montague's Flame. In his youth, Moor had entered and won. Training himself to enter the race, a grueling test of a Horseman's heart, should be enough to keep his mind off a hopeless romance. Not that he expected to win again. He knew he'd be competing against younger Horsemen, but as long as he finished well, he'd be satisfied.

Dawn broke just as he landed in Kingsville. Several people wandered the streets, caring for animals and opening shops. Moor landed on the large Running Way, careful to avoid Horsemen taking off for early morning flights. Panting a bit from the fast flight, he walked along the Running Way until his body cooled and his sweat-dampened full-coat dried. He strode across the village square to the local jail. The Sheriff was in charge of the race, supplying security and taking names of entrants.

The Sheriff, a gray-coated Horseman with a long, steel-colored moustache, narrowed his eyes at Moor when he asked to enter the race. "You know the average winner is eighteen to twenty one years old?"

Moor's anger bristled. He couldn't fathom why the Sheriff's words annoyed him. He knew he didn't have the endurance of his youth, but he wasn't quite ready to be put out to pasture yet, either.

"What is the age limit?"

"Forty, though I don't know many Horsemen of that age who choose to compete with these crazy youngsters."

"Then I still have four years to go before I'm banished to the Senior Races. Add my name to the list. I'm Moor."

The Sheriff shrugged. "All right. You certainly look strong enough to at least finish. The only other qualification is that you must have either completed two endurance races in the past year or are a Carrier and can prove that, within the past six months, you've completed at least two or more Gatherings within the same day."

"I easily make the second qualification and can supply written proof from my village Chieftain.

"Excellent. Last I need your rider's name."

"Since when do you need a rider to race?"

"This year it's been decided that all entrants must have a rider."

Moor's brow furrowed. "Why?"

"You know how there's always been talk about humans getting in on the competition and that it reflects more skill for a Horseman to complete the race with someone on his back."

"Can you list me and I'll give you my rider's name later?"

"Sorry. I need it now. However, you may change your rider up until the day of the race. Just give me a name."

"Inez," Moor stated. He had no doubt that she would ride him, if necessary.

The Sheriff scrawled both names on a slip of half-filled parchment.

"The entry fee of a hundred silver pieces is due two weeks before the race. Good luck to you."

Moor curled his lip and stalked out of the jail, his jaw taut. Once upon a time, a race like The King Montague's Flame would have been nothing more than a pleasure trip to him. Still, that was a long time ago. Not that he hadn't kept himself in good condition. Only the strongest Horsemen with the greatest endurance flew Gatherings, and he was considered one of the best. At times, he flew as many as two or three flights a day. Few Carriers could fly so many without becoming sick, injured, or tired to the point of danger.

Though the Sheriff was right and he probably *wouldn't* win, where was it written that he *couldn't* win? A few older Horsemen had won The King Montague's Flame in the past, why couldn't he?

Moor lifted his chin as he headed back to the Running Way. He'd begin training immediately, since the two months to the race would pass quickly. He wondered if Susana would watch it—

Was he crazy? He'd signed on so that he could forget about her, now he was wondering if she'd see him race.

At the Running Way, Moor galloped and spread his wings. A long, quick flight was just what he needed, and no more thoughts of the adorable little healer. He needed to speak with Jonis. If he would ride him in the race then Moor wouldn't need to ask Inez.

He traveled swiftly to Jonis's cottage on the outskirts of Hornview. Rather than feeling tired by the extra speed, he felt invigorated. Perhaps it was the reality of the race hitting him. As he landed, he saw, through the open barn doors, Jonis puttering around with tools.

"Jonis," Moor called.

"Moor." The short, wiry human smiled. "Glad you're here. Will you help me a second? I've been building a new bed for me and the missus and need help moving the frame."

Moor stepped inside, lifting the entire frame easily. "Where do you want it?"

Jonis pointed to a corner.

"You know, I have a big favor to ask," Moor said as he placed the bed on the wooden floor.

"What do you need?" Jonis stood facing Moor, his arms folded across his chest.

"I need a rider to race with me in The King Montague's Flame."

Jonis stared for a long moment before he smiled. "The King Montague's Flame, eh? I've watched that race every year since I was a boy. I heard they're requiring riders this year. You're really going to enter?"

"Already have, but I need a rider."

"It's going to be a tough race. Young Horsemen, young riders." Jonis grinned and extended his hand to Moor. "If you'll go for it, I'll go for it."

Moor shook Jonis's hand and returned his smile. "I owe you for this."

"No, I owe you. Never thought I'd be in a race like that and on a damn powerful Horseman."

"Thank you, Jonis. I'm proud to have you on my back."

"When do you want to train? I know you're staying at your brother's."

"I'm going to be there for a while, but I'll come here in the mornings so we can practice."

"Great. The earlier the better. That way the wife can't complain." Jonis winked. "Speaking of the wife, she's going to call me to eat soon. Want to stay around?"

"No, thank you. I'm going to stop by Inez and Terra's."

"See you tomorrow?"

"Early."

The men exchanged salutes before Moor plodded over the hillside toward Inez's. By the time he arrived, he'd cooled down from his flight and actually felt a bit cold in the frosty air.

When he knocked on the door, Terra answered, hitching up his trousers, his long, black hair in disarray.

Moor shifted uncomfortably on his front hooves. "Sorry. This is a bad time, isn't it?"

"A few minutes more and it would have been worse." Inez grinned as she approached, belting her robe around her waist. She leaned against Terra who placed an affectionate arm around her. "I'm only joking, Moor. It's nice to see you. Are you home for good?"

Moor shook his head. "I just stopped by to say hello since I was back in the area. I'm staying with Pete for a while longer." Moor was about to continue when, from the corner of his eye, he caught sight of Susana emerging from the side of the house.

He turned, his heart pounding as their gazes met. For a moment both seemed frozen then Susana's lips flicked upward in a smile and she said, "Moor. I thought you were at your brother's?"

"I just came by to tell Inez and Terra I've entered The King Montague's Flame."

"What?" Inez demanded.

"Have you really?" Terra's ears pricked forward and his eyes held a look of keen interest. "That's quite an endurance race."

"I know. I won it in my youth."

Terra looked impressed. "What made you decide to enter again? Inez never told me you raced."

"That's because I didn't know." Inez reached for Moor's hand and squeezed it. "That's an awfully dangerous race, Moor."

"Yes, it is." Susana approached, standing so close to Moor that their bodies almost touched. "I know why you're doing this."

His pulse raced. She must know how much she affected him. How degrading.

"It's because of the injury from your last Gathering, isn't it?" Susana continued. "You feel you have to prove yourself."

Moor sighed with relief. "That's not it at all. I just need something to keep me occupied this winter. Besides, the race isn't even as dangerous as the Gatherings."

"Just be careful," Inez said.

"Yes, I don't want to be patching you up again any time soon," Susana told him.

"I think it's a great idea." Terra nodded. "You're in excellent condition and with training I'm sure you'll be one of the best Horsemen there, if not the best."

"Thank you. At least someone doesn't think thirty-six is old enough to be put to pasture."

"Hardly." Terra snorted. "In a few years, I'll be there myself."

"Inez, I was just out for a walk and thought I'd stop by for a rest before heading home, but I see it's a bad time," Susana said, her gaze sweeping Terra's bare chest and Inez's robe-covered body.

"No," Terra said. "Would you both like to come in?"

"No, thanks," Moor and Susana spoke together. Their eyes met and they grinned.

His pulse beating in his throat and his belly taut from nerves, Moor managed to ask calmly, "Would you like a ride back to the village?"

Susana's mouth opened then closed before she finally said, "I'm not keen on flying."

"I'll be glad to walk."

"Well—"

"Don't worry, Susana." Inez winked. "He's really gentle. Unless you think Linn might be upset."

"Why would Linn be upset? He and I are good friends, that's all."

"Uh-huh." Inez flashed a knowing look which Susana ignored.

"Yes, I'd like a ride," Susana told Moor.

He walked to a short stone wall that Susana stood on to mount him. They waved goodbye to Inez and Terra as Moor headed for the village square.

The barrage of emotions was almost too much to process. Susana's legs, satiny smooth beneath her dress, hugged his equine sides. Her small hands rested lightly on his shoulders, yet they seemed to sear him with passion.

"How have you been?" Susana asked.

"Well. And you?"

"Well."

For the next few moments, they traveled in silence. Moor suddenly became aware of damp heat seeping through her panties. Gods, she was as aroused as he was. He felt the mad urge to gallop across the fields and leap into a flight that would bring her pleasure only felt between a Horseman and his mate.

"Moor, I ..." Her hands slid down his arms. Her touch sent a shiver down his spine that rippled right through his equine back to his tailbone.

"What?" he asked gently, glancing at her over his shoulder. Their gazes locked and he stopped walking. Moor's desire had reached a fever pitch and he broke into a light sweat, his body heating as if he'd just come from a tropical flight.

"I..." She shook her head then slipped from his back. "I can walk from here."

"Then I'll walk with you."

"No." She placed a hand on his chest. The motion was meant to rebuff him, but her touch lingered, her fingers gripping the muscles and stroking the damp mat of hair.

He covered her hand with his, pressing it so close he knew she must have felt his slamming heartbeat. He bent and she took a step closer, standing on tiptoe. Their lips met and he held her close, lifting her off the ground. Susana clung to his neck, her tongue meeting his. Their mouths parted but they continued covering each other's faces with kisses. Her skin felt so soft, her scent so arousing.

"Oh, Gods." Susana suddenly turned her face away.

Moor stopped kissing her, though he didn't release her. They stared, eye-to-eye, their noses nearly brushing.

"What are we doing?" Susana murmured.

"Nothing," Moor stated flatly, placing her on the ground. He turned, running a hand through his hair. "I'm sorry, Susana. I should never have done that."

"It wasn't only you."

"You know we can't do this."

"Of course we can't."

He extended his hand. "I'll take you home."

"No." She lifted her chin. "I'll walk. Good afternoon, Moor."

He watched, feeling like a lovesick fool, as she trudged over the field, her spine straight.

"Damn," Moor snarled, galloping hard and shooting into the sky. He circled above, watching over Susana until she reached the village. Then he flew toward Pete's farm at as fast as he could.

The ferocity of his flight seemed to eat up some of his rage and confusion. Obviously Susana felt the same for him as he felt for her. How could she be strong enough to deny it when he felt like giving in to all his emotions and desires? If she could ignore their dreams, then so could he. After all, there were hundreds of reasons they should stay apart and only one reason for them to mate. But love was a frustratingly powerful persuasion...

* * * * *

A couple of hours later, Moor landed near his brother's barn where Pete and Silas were stacking wood.

"You left early this morning." Pete's gaze swept Moor's sweat-soaked form. "Go anywhere special?"

Moor paced in front of the barn as his breathing and pulse slowed. "Kingsville."

"Ah," Pete grinned, "finding out the list of entrants for the race this year?"

"No, I was entering."

Pete laughed then his smile faded when he noted Moor's serious expression. "I didn't think you were interested in racing anymore. Don't you have enough to do flying all over the Spikelands?"

"The Gatherings won't start again until after the race. I need something to keep me busy during the off-season."

"You're really going to be in the race?" Silas asked.

"I am."

"I can't wait to see it. Do you really think you can win?"

"It's not about winning, Silas," Pete said. "It's about finishing, right, Moor?"

"It's always an accomplishment just to finish an endurance race, but there's nothing wrong with winning, either."

"Well, it's a good thing you already know how it feels to win. In your youth, you were one of the greatest endurance racers."

Moor didn't miss his brother's implication. Funny he didn't feel as ancient as everyone seemed to think he was. "Thirty-six isn't an old man, you know."

"Never said it was."

"And you're two years older than me."

"Right. And you don't see me entering any races with a bunch of eighteen year olds."

"You never entered a race in your life."

"No speed."

"And not the best endurance, either."

"Well not all of us could be Fighting Carriers. One in the family was more than enough."

"What's that supposed to mean?"

Pete sighed. "Nothing. I just don't know why you have a sudden interest in entering one of the most dangerous races in the world."

"Because I need something to keep me occupied. You have a family. I don't."

Pete narrowed his eyes in Moor's direction before turning to Silas who glanced from his father to his uncle. "Silas, would you take the sledge to the woods? I'll meet you there soon."

"Sure, Dad." Silas disappeared into the barn and moments later emerged with the sledge trailing behind him. The boy glanced at the adults before plodding across the frosty field.

Once Silas was out of earshot, Pete fell into step beside Moor who circled the barn to cool down. "So are you going to tell me about it?"

Moor raised an eyebrow. "It?"

"More specifically, her. Who is she, Moor?"

Moor's pulse quickened. Pete might appear like a big, dumb Horseman, but he was incredibly perceptive. Even as a child, Moor had found his brother's awareness both comforting and annoying. "What do you mean?"

"I mean I've only seen that glassy look in your eyes once before, and that was when you had Anita. No, don't look away. I know you don't want to talk about her, and I usually respect that. Since you got here I've known something has been bothering you. Now that you've gone completely crazy and entered that race, I have no doubt it's to do with a woman. So who is she?"

"She's..." Moor ran a hand through his damp hair and sighed, remembering the passionate kisses he'd shared with Susana in his dreams. "She's someone I can't talk about, someone I can never have."

"Why? Is she already married?"

"No, but she has another Horseman friend. And she's too young for me."

"How young?"

"Twenty-seven."

"Ahh, rubbish," Pete scoffed. "She's not too young for you. A Horseman with your strength and stamina could handle a woman even younger than that."

"Then why do you think I can't handle the race?"

Pete grinned. "Back to the race again. I'm not saying you can't handle it, but it won't be as easy as when you soared through it at eighteen."

"Do I look like a fool? I know it won't be easy, and I don't necessarily intend to win."

"Don't you?"

"Stop it, Pete. Ever since we were boys you've practically read my mind."

"It's not that I read minds. You're just a terrible liar. I know you. You wouldn't enter any race you didn't believe you have a chance of winning."

Moor's fists clenched. "I can't stop thinking about her, dreaming about her."

"Are they shared dreams?"

"I think. After the first dream, I saw her and she didn't seem affected, but she's in a profession where disguising her emotions is often crucial."

"What's her profession?"

"She's a healer."

"I see. Have you seen her since that dream?"

"Yes."

"And?"

"She seemed affected but unwilling to submit."

"How long have you known her?"

"Several years and nothing like this has ever happened between us."

Pete scratched behind his ear. "So you were never even attracted to her?"

"Of course I was attracted to her. She's lovely, but I was able to keep my desire at bay."

"And now these dreams are uncontrollable?"

"Gods, yes." Moor sighed, his pulse quickening just from thinking of her. He longed to speak her name. It was like poetry to his lovesick ears.

"I'm sure it's just as strong for her. Even if she wants to deny it, eventually you'll seek each other out as lovers."

"Not necessarily. If both parties deny the dream sharing, it will dissipate."

"Do you want it to?"

"Yes. No. Shit," Moor hissed through clenched teeth.

"Well," Pete drew a deep breath and released it slowly, "if you and the woman are set on denying the dreams, I can understand your need to enter the race. You're welcome to stay at the farm while you train."

"Thank you, Pete."

"Well, if ever an older Carrier has a chance of winning, it's you. Good luck, Moor. I hope you get what you want."

Moor nodded as his brother followed Silas's tracks to the woods.

"What I want," Moor breathed, gazing skyward. He wanted Susana in his arms or astride his back as they soared across the sky. Better yet, he wanted to lie naked in bed with her, to kiss and hold her and tell her how much he desired her. Compared to denying their dreams, The King Montague's Flame seemed easy.

Chapter Three
Ultimate Fulfillment

Moor leapt over the fence behind Pete's barn, his wings pressed tightly to his sides. He landed without missing a beat and galloped across the field. Part of the King Montague's Flame included two ground races with jumps of different sizes. Wing work was not allowed during the ground sections of the race. All of the Horsemen's power would be in legs alone. Moor's hooves struck the ground in a steady rhythm, the scent of grass most pleasant as he galloped. Though he enjoyed ground work, flying thrilled him most. The last of the race's four legs was a hundred mile flight across an ocean of flesh-eating plants. One rest period was mandatory between the four sections.

Moor turned abruptly and galloped back toward the jump that Silas had raised a bit higher. The boy shouted praise as Moor cleared it. About to continue his training, Moor was distracted by a messenger galloping over on a tall, black true-horse.

The rider stopped in front of the house and leapt off the horse almost before he came to a stop. The animal was breathing heavily, its coat covered in frothy sweat. Whatever message the woman carried seemed urgent.

Together Moor and Silas raced to the house where Lina had already opened the door and stood talking with the messenger.

"What's going on?" Pete hurried out of the barn and joined the small group.

"Moor, there's trouble in Hornview," Lina told him.

"What trouble?" Moor's gaze fixed on the messenger. She was a tall, lithe woman with black hair and blue eyes.

"I'm Phillipa, Terra's sister." Of course. She had her brother's eyes. "A Horseman named Kraig has abducted Inez and flown her to the Spikelands where he means to kill her."

"What?" Moor roared. He was going to tear Kraig apart.

"It's some sort of plot against her and Terra. Terra's gone after her, but he's just returned from several rough journeys to the tropics. We're not sure if he'll make it to the Spikelands, and if he does he might not have the strength to fly home with Inez. They both could die out there. There are more details, but we don't have time now. Susana sent me for you. She said you would be able to help."

"I'm on my way." Moor glanced at his brother, Lina, and Silas. "I'll be back when I can."

"Be safe," Lina said.

"And careful," Pete added.

"Good luck, Uncle Moor."

"As soon as my horse is rested, I'll return to the village," Phillipa said, approaching the blowing stallion and stroking his neck.

Noting the woman's concern, Moor said, "Hurry and get on me. I'll fly you."

"I'll take care of your horse." Pete took the stallion's reins.

Gratefully, Phillipa mounted Moor. Moments later, they sped toward Hornview. Memories of Anita's death plagued him. The last time he'd been summoned for a loved one in trouble, he hadn't arrived in time.

He clenched his teeth as his wings pounded the cold winter air.

A short time later, they landed on the Running Way. Susana awaited them. Phillipa dismounted quickly and rushed to the longhouse as Moor cantered toward Susana. Bruises marred her face and she talked so fast he could scarcely comprehend what she was saying.

"Slow down." He grasped her shoulders gently, staring into her frantic eyes. He tenderly touched her black-and-blue cheek. "What the hell happened?"

"Kraig attacked Inez and me at her house. He took her and flew off. He said he was taking her to the slave traders on Blanchard Isle. Oh, Gods, it's all my fault."

Blanchard Isle. Moor's belly sank . It was the most desolate, disgusting place in the tropics, home to the most foul flesh traders in the world. They abducted Horsemen and humans alike, selling them to terrible places such as the mines in the Vertue Mountains. Moor's stomach twisted when he thought of Inez among such filth.

"What do you mean it's your fault?" Moor narrowed his eyes. Susana would never willingly harm anyone, especially her friends.

"Terra was called to serve on the Gatherings in the tropics and arrived home just after Kraig left. He had a bad time of it on the Gatherings, but he flew right back to the tropics after Kraig when I said they were headed for Blanchard Isle. Oh, Moor, Kraig wasn't really going there, it was just a ploy to send Terra away. He's taken her to the Spikelands and plans to kill her unless Terra rescues her."

Moor's pulse raced with rage and fear. He was going to kill that redheaded son-of-a-bitch. How painfully he did it would only depend on whether or not Inez was still alive when he found her.

"Phillipa said Terra has already followed her, but he needs help," Moor said, heading for the tack house. If he was going to the Spikelands, he'd need some quick preparation.

"He no sooner landed from the tropics than he left for the Spikelands. So many flights without rest have taken their toll on him, Moor." Susana swallowed hard as she shook her head. "I don't know if he can make it, let alone save her."

She was right. Moor imagined how sore and tired Terra must be after so many fast flights through severe heat and cold. "I'll find them."

They stepped into the tack house, the familiar scent of soap, leather, and ointment heavy on the air. Anxiety and rage filled him with boundless energy. He reached for his light riding saddle and dropped it on his back. The sticky leaf of a Darrion Plant pinched fur and flesh as he placed it across his nose to ensure clear breathing during the long, fast flight to come. Susana placed blankets in his saddle packs.

An odd feeling stabbed his belly when her small hand settled gently on his equine back. "Please be careful."

He turned to her and extended his hand. She slipped into his embrace, seeming unhindered by the dampness of his full-coat, sweaty from his flight. Affection for her that he could no longer deny or disguise flooded him. His arms tightened around her and he kissed the top of her head. "I won't come back without them. I promise. When I get my hands on Kraig, he's a dead Horseman for what he's done to my daughter and to you."

"Just be careful." Susana lifted her face to his. He bent so their lips almost touched. Her breath mingled with his. Her aroma, herbal with a hint of rose, pierced the pungent tack house scents.

They stepped apart just as Linn burst inside, panting from his flight from the Hall of Fighting Carriers. By the wild look in his eyes and the dampness of his full-coat, he'd answered the cry for help as quickly as Moor.

"What's happened, sweetheart?" Linn strode to Susana and took her hand.

Moor pinned his ears in anger. He wished to hold her hand, but she was with Linn instead. Still, his irritation at seeing Susana and Linn together paled compared to his worry for Inez and Terra.

He finished preparing for his flight as Susana explained the situation to Linn. Moments later, the three emerged from the tack house and headed for the Running Way where the Horsemen would begin their frantic flight northward. Suddenly they caught sight of Terra flying in, his pattern erratic as he headed for a crash landing.

Moor and Linn galloped as fast as they could to where Inez rolled across the hard ground after being flung off Terra who collapsed on his side. Inez must have been badly bruised from the fall, but she scrambled to her husband. As Moor knelt behind her and gathered her into his arms, he noted with concern Terra was bleeding from the nose as well as coughing blood, a condition that occurred when a Horseman's lungs become affected from flying past his physical limits. In the frigid weather, steam rose off his full-coated body.

Inez looked up at Moor with tear-filled eyes. Her sorrow and fear squeezed his heart, reminding him of the orphaned ten year old child he'd met so many years ago.

Neither of them indulged their emotions, however. Not when Terra was in desperate need of help.

Susana arrived with her bag of healing supplies and knelt by Terra to examine him. Moor admired the calm, organized manner in which the little healer took control of the situation. If anyone could save Terra's life, he was sure Susana would do it.

* * * * *

Half an hour later, with Moor and Linn's help, Terra was settled by the fire in the longhouse, Inez beside him. Susana had treated him with herbs and managed to suppress the violent cough, though she could not proclaim him out of danger.

With the initial excitement over, Linn made a hasty apology, saying if he was no longer needed, he must return to the Hall of Fighting Carriers where he had recently been given the position of an assistant instructor. Susana and Inez thanked him for coming, knowing it hadn't been easy for him to get leave on such short notice. Susana thought she'd want Linn's support after the horrible occurrences of the day, but to her shock, she didn't miss him much. Her attention focused on Moor who remained by Terra and Inez. As the women worked to see to Terra's health and comfort, Moor was a tremendous help in repositioning the heavy Carrier when necessary. As she worked, Susana cast glances in his direction when she could. Every now and then, his shoulder would brush hers due to the small space in which they worked. The solid warmth of his body filled her with desire, as did the hushed tones of his deep voice. Only when Inez settled beside her husband for the night, did she and Moor step out of the longhouse.

Susana followed him as he headed for the Running Way.

"Moor."

He turned, his jaw taut. "Yes?"

"Where are you going?" Susana stopped in front of him, staring into his furious amber eyes.

"I'm going to find Kraig."

"But he's probably long gone."

"I have to try. One way or the other, he must be found and made to pay for what he did."

Susana knew from his expression he wouldn't change his mind. Though she hated to admit it, she agreed with him. Kraig needed to be brought to justice. The redhead terrified her. She still felt his fist smashing her face as he knocked her aside after rendering Inez unconscious. He was dangerous and needed to be stopped.

"Please be careful." She grasped his hands.

Tugging her close, he kissed her forehead. His soft lips caressed her skin and the scent of him, musky and wild, shot through her entire body. "I'm so sorry I wasn't here when you and Inez needed me."

"It wasn't your fault." She cupped his cheek, her thumb stroking his stubbled jaw. Gods, he was so handsome, such a perfect specimen of raw male beauty. How could she live in the same village as him and continue denying their attraction?

"Take care of Terra and Inez," he said.

"Kraig's faster than you, Moor."

"I know, but his speed will run out before my endurance does."

Before she could reply, he kissed her mouth then broke into a gallop toward the Running Way. He ascended, his darkly furred body almost invisible in the nighttime sky.

Susana sighed and walked back to the house. Though she had no doubt that if he found Kraig, Moor would beat him in a fight, there was no guessing where the red-haired Horseman had flown after he'd left Inez to die in the Spikelands.

Susana shuddered at the thought of what might have happened to her friend and what still could happen to Terra. The Fighting Carrier had been near death when he'd landed, yet it had been incredibly touching that he risked everything to save the woman he loved. Susana wondered how it would feel to be loved so much. A shiver ran down her spine when she realized she was probably about to find out. The emotions sizzling between her and Moor could no longer be denied.

Back at the longhouse, Susana checked on Terra and Inez before retiring to her room. Unable to sleep, she lay in bed, staring out her small window facing the Running Way. Where was Moor? Had he somehow managed to find Kraig so the bastard could be brought to justice? Here she lay, warm in her bed, while Moor was out there somewhere, flying through wind and ice, probably all for nothing.

Finally she drifted off only to awaken several hours later to the sound of distant hoof beats and shouting. Blinking hazy eyes, she noticed that Moor had landed on the torch-lit Running Way. A man struggled in his grip as the Carrier dragged him toward the village square.

Susana leapt out of bed, splashed water on her face and rinsed her mouth with water and mint leaves to wake herself up. She pulled on boots and shrugged on her cloak over her nightclothes. Cold air struck her as she rushed out of the longhouse, she glanced once toward Inez and Terra who still slept by the fire.

She raced toward Moor who had just stepped out of the guards' barracks. His red-tinged eyes flashed with rage. Steam emanated from his sweaty coat in the cold winter air. His man-chest and equine sides heaved as he caught his breath.

"What happened?" she demanded.

"I couldn't find Kraig. I searched almost every village in the north and went as far as the tropics, though I didn't have time for much questioning there."

"The tropics," Susana snapped. He'd covered a ridiculous number of miles in the few hours he'd been gone. No wonder he looked a bit worn. "Are you trying to end up like Terra?"

He waved his hand. "There's nothing wrong with me."

She followed him towards the tack house, noting he did appear sound. His breathing had slowed to almost normal and his legs looked strong, his movements solid. His scent was so sensual and male. Susana imagined tearing off her clothes and clinging to his hot, damp, powerful body. Her pulse quickened at the thought.

"The bastard is hiding well," Moor continued. "And have you noticed our Chieftain's own Captain of the Guard seems to have disappeared, too?"

Susana's brow furrowed. He was right. Even earlier, when it was announced that Kraig had kidnapped Inez, the Captain had kept his distance, though handling such a crime would normally involve the Chieftain's guards rather than Fighting Carriers.

"The Captain and Kraig have been pilfering Rock Blood from this village's supply as well as from surrounding villages. They've been selling it to traders and making a profit from the wealthy humans purchasing extra shares illegally."

Susana's chest tightened with fury that matched the rage glowing in Moor's eyes. People like Inez, Terra, Linn, and Moor risked their lives to harvest Rock Blood. Kraig and the Captain had been stealing from them all.

"How did you find this out?" Susana's brow furrowed as she watched him toss a blanket and saddle over his back. "And what are you doing now?"

"There's a cave a few miles outside of the village. On my way home, I stopped there on a hunch. I found a trader waiting to contact Kraig. He's the one I just brought to the guards. After some *convincing*, he told me what's been going on with the Rock Blood. I thought Kraig would be returning to the cave, but the trader said he was already gone. If you can believe what scum like that says, Kraig told him he wouldn't be returning to Hornview again. Still, I'm flying a couple of the guards to the cave to watch it in case Kraig returns after all."

"Which guards?" Susana pushed his hands aside and fastened the saddle girth while he used a towel to dry his face and chest. He slipped on a harness for his front passenger to hold during the flight. "I'm not sure who we can trust, considering their Captain has turned out to be a criminal, not that I'm surprised. He always had a sneaky manner."

"Lev and Robert are the guards I'm taking."

Susana nodded. She'd known both for years and trusted them far more than she had ever trusted their Captain.

"I have to tell the Chieftain what went on." Moor strode out of the tack house.

Susana walked beside him, so close that the heat of his body seeped into her. She resisted the urge to stroke his damp coat and hard, sleek muscles.

Together, they entered the longhouse and tapped on the door to the Chieftain's private chamber. The gravel-voiced older man appeared, looking sleepy. Upon seeing Moor, he snapped awake and invited them inside. Quickly, Moor explained the situation. The Chieftain followed them out of the longhouse to the barracks where he intended to question the Rock Blood trader himself.

Lev and Robert had just stepped outside when Moor and Susana arrived with the growling, ranting Chieftain.

"Is the cave far?" Susana asked with concern as the two men mounted Moor. After such a long flight he was bound to be tired. The weight of two guards, not light riders such as Gatherers, wouldn't be easy for an extended trip.

"Not at all. I'll be back in a few minutes." His gaze fixed on hers before he headed for the Running Way.

Susana remained outside for a moment, her arms wrapped around herself against the night chill. With so many horrible things happening, she wondered if life would ever return to normal. Smiling slightly, she had to admit that not everything was so terrible. The giddy, sensual feelings that bubbled inside her whenever Moor was around were far from terrible. They were just complicated, mostly because of her involvement with Linn. It was funny how she fancied herself in love with the younger Horseman. That was until the real thing struck her like water through a broken dam.

Back at the longhouse, Susana checked on Terra and Inez. The injured Fighting Carrier was still deeply asleep from the strong herbal mixture she'd given him earlier. Inez also slumbered close to her husband. Susana was glad her friend was able to sleep, though part of her wished she was awake so they could discuss Moor's discovery.

The thought of people in their own village willing to go to such lengths to steal and attempt murder made her quiver inside. When Moor had arrived, she'd felt safe, much safer than when she was in the longhouse protected by the Chieftain's guards. His guards. The Captain had been as bad as any common criminal. Worse. He'd hidden behind his position and so had Kraig. They knew no one would question either a working Carrier or the village's head of law enforcement entering the storage houses at any time.

Wrapped in her cloak, Susana lingered by the longhouse doors until she heard wings beating overhead. A moment later,

Moor landed on the Running Way. She hurried to meet him. He appeared hot and tired, but no less furious than before.

"I looked for the Captain after I dropped Lev and Robert at the cave. He was nowhere to be found. I take it you haven't seen him in the square?" Moor asked as he headed for the tack house to remove his gear. Pausing at the well, he splashed water on his face and chest.

"The last I saw of him was just before Terra landed. He disappeared after that."

"Bastard," Moor snarled, tearing off his harness, saddle, and blanket. He slammed them over a trunk to dry. "He and Kraig probably escaped together once they realized Terra and Inez survived the flight."

"I wouldn't doubt it."

He sighed deeply, squeezing his temples. "Why wasn't I here? Why was I so damn selfish, leaving this place so I could wallow in self-pity and not face the one person who..."

He paused, swallowing, as his gaze fixed on hers. Susana's heart fluttered in her breast. Did he mean what she thought he meant? He had to be as attracted to her as she was to him. Otherwise, life would be unbearable.

"Moor, you can't blame yourself." She touched his arm. His heat seeped into her hand and flooded her entire body. "You had no idea this was going to happen. Inez is safe and there's a good chance a Horseman as strong as Terra will fully recover."

"Gods, I hope so. Other than Inez, that man's entire life revolves around his speed and stamina. If he can't fly again...I don't even want to think about it. I can't imagine not being able to fly as fast and far as I want."

"You need to cool down." Her gaze swept Moor's damp body. Even disheveled from flight, he made her tingle with desire. The full-coat covered his well-muscled man-torso. His solid yet graceful equine-half exuded power. How she longed to touch him, hold him, feel his mouth on hers. "Would you like some company on your walk?"

"Yes. Very much."

Together they strolled towards the tack house and began circling it. Susana couldn't keep from staring at him. "I..." she began, her voice drifting and her pulse racing. He turned sharply, staring into her eyes. Finally she found her voice and said, "May I stroke you?"

He swallowed, his amber eyes aflame. "Yes. Please."

She lifted her hand and rested it on his equine shoulder. He felt damp, his body hot from his journey. Veins created an intricate pattern beneath his velvet brown coat. His walk slowed as her palm swept down his back and rested on his flanks. She stroked his hindquarters.

"You are so beautiful," she whispered.

He stopped behind the tack house. "No, you are."

Breathing deeply, her heart racing, she ran both hands over his side and equine chest until she stood in front of him. His man-torso was covered in the full-coat, the muscles beneath hard and perfectly formed. The wind whistled through the distant trees as if urging them to fulfill their passions. Susana couldn't control her attraction to him, the love she felt growing stronger each moment they spent together. As she caressed his firm belly, it twitched and tightened beneath her touch. Her hands gripped his solid chest, then grasped his curved biceps.

"Moor?"

"Yes?"

She swallowed. "This is too hard."

"You mean—"

"Being together."

"I want you, Susana. I won't lie about it. I can't." He reached for her, his hands stopping just shy of grasping her upper arms. He curled them into fists and turned away, cursing. "Gods, I want to touch you so much it's almost unbearable."

"It is for me, too." Susana took a step closer and flung her arms around his waist, pressing her face to his chest. The full-coat felt soft, sleek, and wet beneath her cheek. His scent was the wonderful combination of man and horse, leather, sensual musk, and clean sweat. His heart throbbed beneath her cheek. She couldn't imagine not having him as a lover and marveled that they had been able to restrain themselves for this long.

He embraced her tightly. "They say the dreams bring together lovers who are meant to be. I know it's true."

"Yes, because of your wife." She'd always sympathized with Moor's loss, knowing how painful Anita's death had been for him. She thought she might have been jealous talking about her, but for some reason she wasn't. Perhaps because she knew, deep inside, she was meant for him as much as Anita had been. She didn't want to take Anita's place, but to have her own place in his heart.

"I wanted to stay away from you for many reasons. Because you're too young for me."

She chuckled. "Nonsense."

"Because of your relationship with Linn."

Her smile faded. "That might be a problem. I'll have to talk to him, think of a way to tell him, if we decide to act on our shared dreams. He's been a good friend."

"The last reason is fear." Moor took her face in his hands. "Losing Anita nearly destroyed me. I don't want to lose you, too."

Susana's fingers gripped his chest, her gaze burning into his. How she wanted to bare her feelings to him, but no words seemed strong enough. She was a healer, a woman of action. Conveying emotions this deep was strange to her, yet her heart demanded she do so. "I don't want to lose you either, but we can't know what will happen in the future. All I know is that I want to enjoy every moment I can with you."

"I'm already lost to you." Moor swept her into his arms. She clung to his neck as his gaze seemed to grasp her very soul. "I love you, Susana."

"I love you, too." Excitement and tenderness washed over her. This was what she'd longed for all her life. A Horseman who was truly hers, a lover to whom she could give her heart. She tightened her grip on him and kissed his upper lip then his lower.

"Let me finish cooling down, then I can switch to Huform and make love to you."

"Make love?" She offered a mischievous smile.

"The truth?" His deep voice sounded even huskier than usual. "I want to fuck your beautiful body until you scream with pleasure."

Susana's belly tightened and her nipples hardened beneath her robe.

"Meet me in my room when you're ready?" she whispered.

He nodded, taking her hand and kissing the back of it. Tingling with anticipation, Susana drew a deep breath and hurried to the longhouse. In her room, she rekindled the fire and readied her bed for lovemaking with Moor. She heard coughing from the main hall. As the painful, grating sound worsened, she prepared another herbal drink for Terra just as tapping sounded on her door.

"Susana," Inez called.

Susana opened the door and met Inez's worried gaze. She rested a hand on her friend's shoulder. "I'm preparing more tea for him. I'll bring it right out."

"Thank you. He's bleeding again."

"It will only take another minute. Have you gotten some more warm cloths for his chest?"

"Yes, but it's not helping much."

"The tea will let him sleep."

Inez left Susana to prepare the tea. Moments later, a crash sounded from outside. Susana, carrying the tea, hurried to the main hall. Inez, a stunned expression on her face, stood near

Terra who coughed fitfully. Nearby, the Captain of the guard lay dead on the floor, a knife protruding through his chest.

* * * * *

"I don't believe this night." Susana flopped into her bed, rubbing her tired eyes.

In Huform, Moor squatted by the fire, poking the flaming logs with an iron. He had to agree that the night's events were more than unsettling. "I just thank the Gods that Inez and Terra are all right."

"I know." Susana sighed. "I'm glad Inez was able to act in time."

Just an hour ago, Moor had been summoned urgently to the longhouse where Inez had killed the Captain of the Guard. He had returned to the longhouse to kill Terra, also proving that his and Kraig's vendetta would only end in death.

Though Moor was proud of his foster daughter's ability to defend herself as well as those she loved, he knew killing the guard had scarred her emotionally. She was a loving, good woman and killing would not sit well with her.

"I'd planned on returning to my brother's for a while," Moor said, "but I've changed my mind. Not only am I concerned that Kraig will return to finish his job on Inez and Terra , but I can't leave you."

Susana's gaze followed him as he approached the bed and sat on the edge of it, stroking hair from her face. He gently kissed her bruised cheek. She was so soft, so human. The thought of anyone harming her twisted his insides. "And when I think about Kraig lifting a hand to you, I want to kill him."

"Forget about him." Susana locked her arms around Moor's neck. "I've had enough killing and enough abduction to last a lifetime. I don't want to talk about Kraig anymore. Not tonight."

Moor nodded, holding her close and kissing the top of her head.

"Make love with me, Moor."

Without a word, he pressed her onto the mattress and covered her mouth with his. She tasted of heat and lust cooled by crushed mint. The scent of her skin, part natural musk, part floral soap, both soothed and aroused him. Her warm, soft breasts pressed against his chest as one of his legs settled between hers.

Arching closer, she thrust her pelvis against his hip. After his frantic flight halfway around the world, Moor should have felt at least a little tired, but with Susana in his arms, fatigue disappeared, crushed by the drives of his body.

Closing his eyes, he deepened the kiss. His tongue parted her lips as hers—slippery and sensual—met his with matching desire. Small fingers threaded through his hair and caressed his nape. His pulse leapt. He'd had women since Anita had died, but none whom he loved. The sensation was achingly familiar yet completely fresh. Emotion threatened to choke him, so he sought release in the only way he could while retaining his masculine dignity. He lost himself in her lips and touch. At that moment, nothing existed but Susana. His tongue probed slowly, deeply, yet with all the gentleness he could muster. All that mattered was pleasing her. His joy would spring from hers. It was the only way he knew how to make love to a woman as special as this young healer.

"Oh, Moor. I've wanted this for so long." Her words filled him with affection and lust. Soothed by her delicate touch, but impassioned by the heat of her soft, fragrant body, he was lost in an experience even more powerful than the dreams.

Reluctantly, he drew his mouth from hers and touched his lips to her temple. The sensation was no less marvelous. Her smooth, baby-fine hair carried the scent of herbs. It caressed his lips as he kissed the top of her head. Brushing pale wisps behind her ear, he traced the delicate lobe with the tip of his tongue before taking it between his teeth and nibbling tenderly.

She giggled when he buried his face in her neck, licking and kissing the smooth, delicate column.

"I need you so much, Moor." She caressed his shoulders and gripped his back. While he tugged down her dress and licked the hollow between her shoulder and neck, she wiggled beneath him.

Damn the clothes. He wanted her naked curves pressed so close to his body that he couldn't tell where he ended and she began. Grunting with annoyance and desire, he stood and yanked off his boots. His trousers followed.

All the while Susana's large, pale eyes swept him from face to ankle. Her gaze fixed on his cock. It stood out, stiff and eager, though he had no intention of hurrying. It seemed like he'd waited forever to truly hold her in his arms and he wanted to savor every moment. Susana lifted her dress and flung it over her head, revealing her small yet sensuously curved body. Moor drew a sharp breath, his cock throbbing at the sight of her. Firelight flickered off her pale skin. Her nipples stood out, fine little peaks on perfectly rounded breasts. The gentle swell of her belly rested above a neat thatch of honey-colored hair. Sitting on the edge of the bed, Moor gently slid his fingers through the silken curls between her smooth thighs.

Susana shivered and climbed atop him. Moor guided her legs around his waist, loving the sensation of her flesh against his palms. Placing his forearms and palms flat against her back, he kissed first one shoulder then the other. Her skin was so smooth beneath his callused hands. The soft, pleasured sounds escaping her throat heightened his desire. At the first brush of her moist lips across his chest, his eyes slipped shut. The tip of her tongue drew random shapes across the hard planes of muscle as her hands caressed his back and stroked his sides. This was better than his daydreams, better than the shared dreams. Gods, he could scarcely stand the pleasure. It had been so long since he'd kissed and caressed a woman he loved.

"Let me touch you." Susana whispered, using her small strength to push him onto his back. He let her have her way and fell onto the mattress. Her knees braced on each side of his waist, she loomed over him, her hair tickling his face, shoulders, and chest as she covered his torso with kisses.

Moor's heart throbbed wildly. Her marvelous lips and tongue roamed over his taut abdomen, traveling lower until her breath fanned the head of his cock.

At that moment, he stopped breathing and waited, his entire body tense. Suddenly her warm, wet mouth engulfed the crown of his erection. He gasped, trying to avoid making too much noise, since they didn't want to disturb Inez and Terra. The sensation of being sucked and licked by a woman he'd spent weeks dreaming about was overwhelming. Never in his life had he experienced such perfection.

He considered himself an intelligent man, yet at that moment he felt completely stupid and could think of nothing to say except, "Gods, Susana. Ah. Gods."

As she continued swirling her tongue over his cockhead and using the tip of it to trace the underside, he was certain he felt her smile. She licked him from head to root and back again while he did his best to keep from thrusting hard against her face. His fingers nearly tore apart the headboard when she clasped his rod and began sucking the head fast and hard.

Shivers of desire ran down his spine as he grasped her shoulders and tugged her away before he exploded in her soft, slippery mouth.

"Come here," he growled, pressing her onto her back.

She gasped as he laved first one nipple then the other. Parting her thighs with one hand, he circled her pussy with a finger. She was hot and slick to the touch—more than ready for him. Stroking her dark blonde curls with his fingers, he rolled his thumb inside her. He stroked it over her swollen clit. Susana panted, thrusting her pelvis against his hand.

"Oh, Moor." she gasped, clutching handfuls of his hair. His lips fastened on one of her nipples. As he sucked and licked, his thumb toyed with her clit.

An orgasm rippled through her. She writhed, doing her best to silence her moans of desire, but in the end he absorbed them with a kiss.

Without moving his lips from hers, he slid his cock into her hot sheath that formed exquisitely to his shape. The flesh squeezed his cock, bathing it in perfection. He groaned, nearly overcome with sensation. Supporting himself with his arms so as not to crush her with his heavy, thickly-muscled Horseman physique, he thrust with long, slow strokes. She uttered contented sounds deep in her throat as his steady rhythm drove her towards another climax.

Moor's pulse skipped with excitement, especially when her small heels sank deeply into the backs of his legs, pressing him closer.

Orgasm tore through her body. Her spasms clenched and released his cock until he could no longer control his movements. He slammed into her, tearing his mouth from hers and gasping. Pressing his lips against his shoulder, he sucked and licked in one spot, making it sensitive. Suddenly her arms stretched downward. Her hands found his Turning Point on his lower back. In a rush of passion so fierce he lost sight and sound and became a creature of feeling alone, Moor cried out. To a Horseman, his Turning Point was as sensitive as his cock. Having both stimulated provided the most exquisite orgasm any man could hope for.

Rolling onto his back, Moor gathered Susana close. Panting, they lay entangled in each other's tingling, heated bodies.

"Susana, I love you," Moor whispered against her hair.

"I love you, too." She lifted her chin and gazed into his eyes. "Moor, what are we going to do?"

"I want to marry you." His grip on her tightened. "Don't deny me, Susana."

"I can't. I want you too badly." She kissed him. Moor buried his hand in her hair and closed his eyes as their tongues met. They explored each other's mouths, tasting and caressing.

When the kiss finally broke, she said, "Before we tell anyone, you have to let me talk to Linn. He's been a good friend and I don't want him to find out through rumors. I owe him that much."

"Of course."

"I know it's been trying for him at the Hall of Fighting Carriers, this being his first time as an instructor, so I don't want to bother him there, if we can avoid it. In two weeks, he has leave and I'm cooking dinner for him. Do you think we could wait until then?"

Moor's anger bristled a bit at having to wait so long to announce their plans, but she was right. Linn obviously had feelings for Susana and he was a decent Horseman. He was willing to give Linn the same respect he'd want for himself. Just because he and Susana were in love didn't mean the whole world floated in the same dream. Linn's assignment was difficult. There was no need to fly to the Hall and announce their engagement.

"If you don't want to wait, we can tell him sooner," she said.

"No." He stroked her hair. "It's only two weeks. We can handle that."

Susana's eyes gleamed. "To me it seems like forever, but I don't want to spring it on him while he's working. He's been so intense about this assignment."

"Becoming an assistant instructor for the Fighting Carriers is quite an honor, especially since he's only a recent graduate. He's an excellent flyer. Lots of speed."

"Speaking of speed, how's the training for your race?"

"It's going well, even though it's not completely about speed."

"I know. It's endurance. I can't wait to see you at the finish."

Elation coursed through him. "You're going to watch? I thought you might be too busy with your work."

"I wouldn't miss it."

"If you have time, maybe you could help me practice?"

"How?"

"I train daily and could use you on my back. Jonis only has the mornings to practice."

Susana drew a deep breath, her smile fading. She rolled onto her side and gazed at the fire.

"Susana? What's wrong?"

"You know I've never flown on a Horseman."

Moor grinned grasping her waist and tugging her on top of him. He gyrated his hips teasingly. "There's nothing to it."

"I mean it, Moor." She tugged away. "I'm afraid of flying."

His mirth faded when he realized the intensity of her distress. He stroked her shoulder with his fingertips. "I'm sorry. I didn't mean to offend you."

"You didn't." She turned, her gaze fixed on his. "I'm sorry for snapping at you. I've always been able to avoid flying with Linn, but since you and I...I guess I have to."

"You don't have to do anything." Moor cupped her chin in his hand. "I love you, Susana. If you never want to fly with me, that's fine. I'm not saying it wouldn't be nice, but there's more to life than that."

"The funny thing is, I want to fly with you. I never really wanted to fly with Linn, that's what made saying no so much easier."

"Would you like to try?"

She looked hesitant. "I...I would, but the thought of leaving the ground. I don't know if I could do it."

"I think once you do, you'll love it. It's so beautiful up there, Susana. You can see everything. There's such a feeling of freedom. There's no way to express it. It's something that must be experienced."

"I want to, but what if I fall?"

Moor took her hands and held them to his chest, his gaze fixed on hers. "I won't let you fall."

* * * * *

Susana stared at Moor, her heart pounding. Gods, she did want to fly with him, but she'd always been so afraid of heights. Could she get over it to share the splendor she'd only heard about?

"All right," she stated. The best way to get over fear was to confront it. If she wanted to fly with Moor, she needed to jump in and do it.

"You want to try?"

"Yes. Unless you're too tired."

"You mean now?"

"Before I change my mind."

Moor stood and swept her into his arms. Before setting her on her feet he kissed her and said, "Get on some warm clothes. It gets cold up there, especially in wintertime. Once I get warmed up, I'll be hot enough to keep you comfortable, but until then I don't want you getting chilled."

Susana opened the trunk at the foot of her bed and removed trousers and a shirt she sometimes used when traveling between villages. As she dressed, her hands and belly quivered with apprehension and excitement. This was it. She was really going to fly. Moor pulled on his trousers and boots.

They donned cloaks and walked to the tack house. Inside, Moor undressed again and stepped into another room to change to his equine-half. Though she'd seen him and other Horsemen change before—usually when they were ill—most preferred privacy when shifting shape. She understood why. Many humans thought the seconds when they molded from two legs to four or vice versa, was ugly. While Susana didn't find the changing particularly attractive, it didn't offend her, and the end result was stunning.

The floor trembled beneath her feet. Moments later, Moor emerged from the back room with his sleekly-muscled equine-half. Susana's gaze swept him, admiring his powerful muscles beneath a gleaming brown full-coat. His brown wings pressed to his sides.

"You're so gorgeous." She reached out a hesitant hand towards his equine back, then gazed at him in question, as if awaiting the signal to stroke him. Proper etiquette dictated that a Horseman not be stroked without permission.

"You never have to ask," Moor said, as if reading her mind. "I'm yours."

A smile tugged at her lips as she ran both hands down his side and over his rump. The muscles were hard and lean. Power emanated from both his man and horse halves. She knew what it felt like on his back, but not when they were sailing across the sky. Her fingers trailed over his wings, the feathers velvety soft.

"Are you sure you're all right?" he asked.

"Yes. Why?"

"Your hands are shaking."

"I'm nervous."

"Don't be." He took her hand and kissed the back of it. The hair on his face tickled her flesh. Most women either found a full-coated Horseman incredibly sexy or completely offensive. She couldn't imagine the latter.

The full-coat lent an air of primitive beauty to Moor's handsome appearance. His facial features and man-torso were covered in the same short, sleek brown coat as his equine-half, making his amber eyes seem even lighter. The pointed tips of his ears flickered a bit as he smiled at her, his teeth gleaming against his dark face.

Reluctantly, he released her hand and approached his trunk at the end of the tack house. He opened it, removing his blanket, saddle, and harness.

Susana placed the blanket on his back before he dropped the saddle on. While she tightened the girth, he slipped the harness over his man-torso and fastened it.

"When we go up, you might feel more secure if you hold on to me instead of using the harness."

"That's not the proper way to ride, though, is it?"

He cast her a roguish grin. "It is for us. Flying with a lover is far different than flying with any other rider."

"I've heard." Susana's face heated. Since the beginning of time, stories had circulated about the gratification Horsemen provided their lovers while in midair. Susana had dreamed of it, but never really believed it would happen to her.

Outside, she mounted Moor. He grinned at her over his shoulder as she slid her fingers into the grips on his harness. "I won't go high until you're comfortable. As soon as you want to come down, just let me know."

She nodded, since fear had stolen her voice. Trembling from more than the cold, she thought she must be crazy.

"Don't be afraid," he told her.

She was a healer, damn it. She dealt with life and death every day. She'd be damned if she was going to succumb to a fear of heights and destroy what would be a meaningful part of her relationship with Moor.

"Go ahead. I'm fine."

Moor walked to the Running Way. Gradually he increased his pace until he cantered up and down the long stretch. Susana clung to him hard, so terrified that she sat stiffly in the saddle. Her teeth jounced with every thud of his hooves.

"I'm going to gallop," he said.

"I'm fine down here," she said. "It's going up that bothers me."

"Don't worry. Just hang on. Don't let me go."

"I'm not about to."

Gripping the saddle with her knees, she pressed close to his man-half as he broke into a gallop, his long, powerful legs swallowing ground.

"Ready?" he shouted.

"Do it."

"Hold me tight."

Susana's hands slipped from the grips and she wrapped her arms around his chest.

Though it seemed impossible, his speed increased even more as she held him fiercely, her cheek pressed against his back. Though she hoped she didn't impede his breathing, she was too afraid to loosen her grip. His wings spread around her, beating the air. It was about to happen. She was really going to fly. Terror and excitement filled her and she felt a bit dizzy.

"Close your eyes and keep holding me," he ordered.

Susana squeezed her eyes shut.

After several moments, he called, "How do you like it?"

Susana opened her eyes, stunned to see that they hovered over the village square. A nervous laugh broke from her throat. His takeoff had been so smooth, she hadn't even realized they'd ascended.

"Susana?" He glanced over his shoulder.

"I'm fine." She pressed close to his back to hide from the cold, breath-stealing wind.

"Want to go higher? There's an annoying draft I'd like to get over."

"All right."

His huge wings pounded the air as they rose. His muscles lurched as his legs churned beneath her. A quick glance below revealed the snowy, moonlit hillside. Terra and Inez's house rolled past, then they were soaring over open fields. The wind howled in her ears. Ahead, the full moon seemed close enough to touch.

As her terror faded, Susana became aware of other sensations. In midair, she was able to relax in the saddle, unlike riding a true-horse over land. The rhythm of Moor's galloping legs seemed to lock onto her pussy. Desire filled her. Now she understood the magical flights Horsemen's lovers spoke of.

Beneath her cheek, Moor's heart beat in a powerful, steady pace through his back. She loosened her death grip on him and stroked his chest, then kissed the center of his back.

"Do you like it?" he asked.

"I love it." What in the world had she been afraid of? This was the most magnificent experience of her life.

"You're doing well. With some more practice, you'll be a terrific rider."

"You think so?"

"My sweet, I know so. Already I don't want anyone else on my back."

Smiling, she hugged him a bit tighter.

After several moments, his speed increased. Susana narrowed her eyes, burying her face deeper in his back. Her heart raced and pussy throbbed to the rhythm of his gallop. His body heated, warming her against the winter night. Still, when they landed on the Running Way, he hadn't even broken a sweat and his breathing was scarcely elevated.

"Would you like me to dismount?" she asked.

He smiled at her over his shoulder. "Not yet. I like you up there. No one's out here at this time of night. Keep holding me."

Susana did as he asked, her arms wrapped loosely around his chest, stroking the rich brown coat over solid muscle.

She giggled. "I flew on a Horseman."

"I knew you'd like it."

"More than like. I can't wait to do it again."

"Tomorrow?"

"I thought you'd never ask."

Susana sighed with pleasure and closed her eyes, her cheek resting against his back. Never in her life had she imagined being so happy with a man. Keeping their relationship discreet for two weeks would be torture. She wanted to announce her love for the marvelous Carrier to the entire world.

Chapter Four
Secret Keepers

Moor snarled as he lifted his ax overhead and swung downward, splitting a log in two and digging halfway through the chopping block as well. It had been a week since Terra and Inez's near fatal flight, a week since he and Susana had made love and entered an incredibly romantic yet secret relationship. He understood the reasons for their silence regarding how they felt about one another, at least until Linn returned and she could tell him the truth. Still, Moor's heart overflowed with love for Susana. The need to announce their affection to the world was almost unendurable.

He bent and picked up the split logs, tossing them into the enormous pile behind his cottage on the edge of the village square. The aroma of wood and cool, damp earth surrounded him. Nothing like fresh air and hard work to ease a man through life's frustrations.

"So do you plan on supplying the entire village with firewood this winter?"

Moor glanced over his shoulder at Terra who stood near the side of the cottage. The Fighting Carrier cocked an eyebrow at the ridiculous amount of split logs. Though he still appeared pale and had lost weight during his illness, Terra's cough had improved and each day he regained strength. Moor hoped the younger Horseman would soon be able to fly again and suffer no long-term effects from his injuries.

"No. I just need the exercise."

"How's the training going for the race?"

"Very well. Jonis and I work together in the mornings and I train in the afternoon, too."

Terra sighed, his gaze fixed on the horizon. "I envy you, Moor. I loved racing."

Moor approached, wiping his forehead with the back of his hand. "You'll race again."

"Yes," Terra's jaw set, "I will. I intend to be ready to fly during the next Gathering Season, and I'd love to enter the sprint in Gray Flats this summer."

"Just concentrate on recovering. You have your whole life to fly." Moor knew his words were of little comfort. Until they were certain Terra's injuries weren't permanent, the man would be on edge. Moor couldn't blame him. Terra's career depended on his speed and endurance. The idea that a useless son-of-a-bitch like Kraig might have ruined a great Fighting Carrier like Terra made Moor ill, though not as ill as knowing Kraig had injured Susana and nearly killed Inez.

Susana. Gods, he couldn't wait until tonight when they could be together. Excitement flooded him, so he picked up his ax and began chopping a thick tree. Within seconds his Horseman's strength had felled the tree and he stood, panting, his human legs braced apart. Sweat seeped through his shirt.

"So what's bothering you?" Terra ventured.

"What makes you think something is bothering me?"

"Because you just cut down that tree like it was an Ice Lizard on the attack."

Moor sighed, leaning his ax against the chopping block. He rubbed his eyes. Keeping his relationship with Susana a secret from those closest to him had proven difficult. Perhaps he could talk about it without giving everything away. He needed to discuss what was happening with someone who understood. Someone like Terra, who also had a dream lover.

"What's the problem?" Terra's brow furrowed.

Moor drew a deep breath and released it slowly. "I've...I've been having dreams."

"Dreams? As in shared dreams?"

Moor nodded.

"Well, that's great...isn't it?"

"Yes and no."

Terra grinned. "When Inez and I shared dreams, I wasn't complaining."

"I've been through this before."

Terra's smile faded. He took a step closer to Moor. "I know. I'm sorry. But can't you think of this as another chance? Many Horsemen never find a dream lover even once. Now you have the opportunity for that kind of love again."

"I know. I'm luckier than I have a right to be."

"So who is she?"

Moor's gaze shifted toward the distant cottage. As if by magic, Susana stepped out of a cottage, her bag of healing supplies slung over her shoulder. His heart fluttered at the sight of her. What he wouldn't give to bound across the field and sweep her into his arms.

Terra's stare switched from Moor to Susana and back again. He tilted his head in the healer's direction, his expression stunned. "You mean...Susana?"

Moor didn't respond, but picked up his ax and hacked another tree. Terra caught his wrist as he lifted his arm to swing.

"It is Susana, isn't it?" the black-haired Horseman pressed. "What about Linn?"

"I didn't say anything, and I think we should end this conversation."

"Does Inez know? Of course not. She would have told me, unless you and Susana swore her to secrecy or something. Even so, she wouldn't be able to keep it from me. I'd know if she was hiding something —"

"I never realized you were so nosy."

Terra looked insulted. "I am not nosy. You're the one who told me about your dream lover."

"Only because you kept pushing me."

"Because you were acting like you had something on your mind. I mean, take a look around." Terra gestured toward the pile of firewood nearly as high as Moor's cottage.

Moor's teeth clenched. Terra was right. He was mad with love. He wanted the entire village to know how he felt about Susana, but he'd promised to keep silent.

"I know you're going to tell Inez about the conclusion you've jumped to, but please keep the information between yourselves."

"Then it's true?"

"Shouldn't you be back at the longhouse resting?" Moor snarled.

"Probably." Terra winked. "But this is more interesting."

"Go. I have work to do."

Terra chuckled as he turned away. "Inez will be looking for me soon. Don't worry, Moor. Your secret is safe with us."

At least Moor was certain of that. Inez and Terra were probably the only people in Hornview who could be trusted not to gossip.

Terra paused and glanced over his shoulder. "Best of luck to you, Moor. You both deserve happiness."

Moor smiled before he turned back to chopping wood.

* * * * *

Moor stood quickly, placing aside the book he'd been trying to read, and answered his door. He was so obsessed with Susana, he'd been unable to concentrate on the book or anything but her, except while training. Only when pushed to his physical limits was he able to focus on something other than their love affair. Speaking with Terra that afternoon had fueled his anxiety rather than eased it. What if Susana was using Linn as an excuse to avoid publicly admitting the dream sharing? Linn was very young, handsome, and at the peak of his power. Though women often commented on Moor's attractive appearance, he was no longer young. Moor had always been aware of his attributes, but he also prided himself in honestly accepting his faults. Youth, he realized, was no longer on his side. He was still a stronger flyer than most Horsemen half his age, but he felt the aftereffects of hard journeys more than he did in his youth.

He opened the door. Susana, wrapped in her cloak, smiled at him.

"I thought I'd never get here," she said, stepping inside. "One of the children on the outskirts fell and broke his arm. I didn't want to leave until I made sure he was all right."

Moor held her close, thoughts of Linn settling to the back of his mind now that she was snug in his embrace. Burying his face in her hair, he inhaled her sweet herbal scent. It felt so good to be close to her again.

Tilting her face upward, she asked, "How was your day?"

"Fine. I had a talk with Terra."

"I had one with Inez." Susana looked a bit guilty. "She guessed about us. I tried not to appear obvious, but…why are you laughing?"

"Terra did the same with me."

"And I've been worried that you'd be mad at me for blabbing." Susana playfully smacked his arm.

"They won't tell anyone else."

"To be honest, I'm glad somebody knows. It's so difficult pretending our feelings for one another haven't changed."

Suddenly Moor's smile faded and his stomach tightened. Inez knew.

Susana's brow furrowed. "What's wrong?"

"How did Inez feel about us being together? Did she seem upset?"

"Not at all. She's…" A knock on the door interrupted her.

Grumbling, Moor opened the door.

Terra and Inez stood outside, looking nosier than he ever remembered.

"We thought we'd ask you to dinner," Inez said.

"Really?" Moor cast them an accusing look while trying to keep an amused smile from his face.

"But you seem to have company," Inez continued, glancing at Susana. "Unless you're sick and need a healer?"

Moor raised his eyes to heaven, grasped Inez's arm, and tugged her inside. Terra followed. "You're two of the worst liars I've ever met."

"Then it is true?" Inez smiled. "You and Susana have shared dreams?"

"It was *not* my idea to come here." Terra held up his hands in mock defense. "But you know Inez once she gets something in her head."

"Inez, huh?" Moor cast Terra a disbelieving look.

"You should know. You raised her."

"And did a damn fine job of it, too," Inez said. "Susana, he'll make a wonderful father."

"We're not even married yet and you already have me pregnant." Susana laughed, then pressed close to Moor's side. "Though it's not a bad idea."

Moor had to admit the thought was appealing. He imagined Susana plump with his child, of holding his daughter in his arms or teaching his son the joys of flying. Still, after what happened with Anita, he was not about to get ahead of himself. It would be more than enough if he could have Susana for the rest of their lives.

"The dinner invitation is still open, if you'd both like to come," Inez said. "Perhaps you can talk Terra out of flying too soon. He's been talking about going up without waiting for Susana's approval."

"What?" Susana snapped at the Fighting Carrier. "I know you're feeling better, but I told you not to even consider flying for at least another week."

"Don't be a fool," Moor agreed. "If you go up too soon, you might have a relapse that will be even more difficult to recover from. You don't want to ruin yourself for life, do you?"

"No." Terra's jaw tightened. "But I'm tired of cantering around like a child's pony."

"Push yourself too soon and that's all you be able to do for the rest of your life." Inez's fists clenched and her eyes flashed with anger and concern.

Moor understood her worry, but he also knew how Terra felt. His health was rapidly returning and staying out of the air must have been torture for him.

"One more week, Terra," Susana said. "Then you can start flying again gradually."

The Fighting Carrier nodded, his teeth clenched visibly as he slammed a fist into his palm. "I hate this. What bothers me even more is that no one's been able to locate Kraig. I know you've been trying harder than anyone, Moor."

It was true. Moor flew almost daily, using his training as an excuse to comb villages and wilderness alike for the elusive criminal. As soon as Terra recovered, they planned to search for him together.

"Yes, and I wish he'd stop for a while." Susana's reprimanding gaze turned from Terra to her lover.

"Someone has to find him," Moor stated.

"One way or the other, our paths will cross again," Terra said. "And when they do, I will kill him."

Moor's teeth ground. "Not before I do."

"All right, that's enough," Inez snapped. "Hasn't there been enough violence around here?"

Susana sighed. "Maybe we should all just sit down to dinner and relax."

"I have stew already cooking," Inez said.

The group stepped outside and walked over the snowy hillside to Inez and Terra's cottage where they shared a meal and, afterward, sat by the fire. No one mentioned Kraig for the remainder of the evening, though Moor knew the others' thoughts must have strayed to the evil Carrier as much as his did.

The moon had risen to its full height when Moor and Susana said goodnight to their friends.

Once outside in the crisp air, Moor took Susana's hand and kissed the back of it. "Would you like a ride?"

Susana stood on her tiptoes and slipped her arms around him. "What do you think?"

Moor's hands slid over her shoulders and back. "What are you wearing under that dress?"

"Nothing," Susana whispered.

"Perfect." Moor closed his eyes and sighed with passion. The thought of her silky thighs pressed naked against his beast back was enough to send shivers of desire down his spine. Even his Turning Point tingled.

He stepped close to a tree stump. "Mount."

* * * * *

Susana's thighs clasped Moor's sides. She relished the smoothness of his coat and the flexing of his enormous muscles as he broke into a canter.

Her hands slipped around his torso, her palms splaying against his thick, rock-hard chest. Gods, he was the most sensual, exciting creature she'd ever known. All her dreams of riding a Horseman came true whenever she slid onto his back. She felt so safe with him that she wondered how she'd ever been afraid of flying.

Still, when so far from the ground, danger was ever present. It only seemed to add to the excitement of flight. In the sky, she was completely at his mercy. Her survival depended on his strength, agility, and willingness to protect her with his life, if necessary.

Moor's pace increased until his hooves barely seemed to touch the ground. Susana's knees hugged his withers as she pressed her chest close to his man-back and listened to his throbbing heartbeat. Her eyes slipped shut as he spread his wings. Gods, she loved the sensation of his powerful body so close to hers and the beating of his magnificent, velvety wings surrounding her. Moments later, the wind grew stronger and she knew they were flying.

Susana smiled and kissed between his shoulder blades, her fingers stroking his chest.

"Would you like to try going a little faster?" he asked. "Believe it or not, faster on one of us up here is much easier than on a true-horse down there."

"I'm game." She tightened her grip on him a bit.

"That's good, but try to relax. Ready?"

"Yes."

The wind whooshed in her ears as his wings beat faster. He bounded across air and a thrill coursed through her. His torso was an excellent shield against the harsh winds, protecting her eyes and skin and making it possible to breathe even while wrapped in his blinding speed.

I've never felt anything like this. She smiled, her entire body tingling. A quick glance below revealed only rolling meadows and patches of forest. Lost in the fast, powerful flight, she had no idea how many miles they covered before she felt him draw a deep breath. In spite of the wind, she was warmed by his body's tremendous heat. His heartbeat throbbed madly as he raced. His flesh grew slick with sweat beneath her cheek and palms, his musky, sensual aroma tantalizing her. Heat and moisture from his damp coat seeped into her bare legs and stimulated her pussy in a way she'd never dreamed possible.

She moaned softly, her fingers kneading the damp mat of hair covering his chest.

"Are you all right?" Moor called above the wind.

"I'm too all right. Gods, it's like making love in midair."

"Then I must be doing it right."

Embarrassment flashed through her but disappeared in the face of far more powerful emotions. She was about to come, unless Moor slowed down or landed very soon.

He didn't. Instead he leapt forward in another burst of speed, sustaining it as his muscles strained and his heart raced. Susana's legs felt weak though they gripped his sides as tightly as her arms clutched his torso. Her eyes closed, she panted nearly as hard as he. This was too much for any woman to endure. It was just too fantastic. Pressure built in her belly. Her clit and pussy ached with need only he could fulfill with every leap of his powerful Horseman body. She throbbed and shivered in the most magnificent and unusual climax she'd ever experienced.

As her arms and legs relaxed, he slowed his flight. Within a moment, his breathing and pulse slowed, a mark of his excellent physical condition. He was a strong Carrier, and Susana had no doubt he'd do well in the endurance race, even when competing against younger Horsemen. She wondered if Moor's years of experience might even give him an advantage over the young, hot-headed stallions. Though she told herself winning didn't matter, deep inside she *wanted* to see him place well.

"We're home." He glanced at her over his shoulder.

Susana looked down at the village square. Moor landed smoothly on the dark Running Way and Susana slid off his back. Her first steps were a bit unsteady. After such a marvelous ride, walking on two human legs seemed a most clumsy way to travel. Grasping her arm, he tugged her close and bent, brushing her lips with his. Susana stood on tiptoe, sliding her arms around his neck. Reluctantly, she let him go. The Running Way was no place for a romantic scene.

"I need to cool down." He stroked her cheek with the back of his hand. "I'll walk you home."

"Do you want me to rub you down?" She gazed at him through her lashes.

"I'd love it, but it's late and you need to be on your rounds early tomorrow."

Susana sighed. He was right. Smiling, she rested her hand on his chest and said, "With all the stories about how wild Horsemen are, I have to end up with a sensible one."

His brow furrowed. "Is that bad?"

"Not at all."

"Why are you looking at me like that?"

Susana's eyes widened. "Like what?"

"This is because you're nearly as young as my daughter. My daughter. By the Gods, what the hell am I doing?" His fists clenched and he began pacing.

What in the world was wrong with him? Susana would never understand the male of any species. Placing her hands on her hips, she stared at him. "Look, Moor, I hate to ruin your self-disgust, but I must say you're not even old enough to be my father. I might be younger than you, but I'm older than Inez and unless you were fathering babies when you were eight years old, you're not old enough to be her blood father, either."

He paused. "You both just seem so young."

"Well, grandfather, maybe Inez and I were right about you not being able to handle the race."

"Not handle... I have news for you, the reason I lead Gatherings is because I can out-fly and out-fight almost every other Horseman in the village. Not only that—why are you laughing?"

She'd known insinuating he was too old for the race would shake some sense into him. A Horseman's grand self-image was usually his greatest downfall. Not that Moor had any cause for real concern about the race. She had no doubt he would do better than most of the entrants. Perhaps he'd even win.

Susana reached for his hand and tilted her face up to his. "I thought you were going to walk me home?"

He growled, tugging her close to his side as they headed for the longhouse.

"Are you coming back to spend the night?" she asked hopefully.

"Do you want me to?"

"Only if you want to."

Say yes, Moor. Please say yes. Nothing would feel better than cuddling with him for the rest of the night.

His lips flickered upward. "I'll be back."

Grasping her shoulders, Moor covered her mouth with his. Susana buried her fingers in his hair, holding him close. She closed her eyes, lost in his gentle kiss.

Slowly, he pulled away and traced the shape of her lips with his fingertip. "See you soon."

"I'll be waiting."

Susana watched from the door as he turned away. Before disappearing around the corner of the house, he smiled at her over his shoulder. Susana's stomach tightened and her heartbeat quickened. Nothing felt as good as being in love.

Chapter Five
In the Bathhouse

The fast flight with Susana had done little to deplete Moor's energy. As he walked across the fields, he resisted the urge to run and even fly again. Being with Susana invigorated him. Feeling her come while riding him had excited him so much he wanted nothing more than to tear off her clothes and bury himself deep in her hot, tight little body. It was late, and both of them needed to wake early, her to work and him to train. Damn. Maybe she was right. He was too sensible. Still, he needed to meet Jonis at dawn to practice.

Though he enjoyed working with his regular rider, he wished Susana would be riding him in the race. It was a crazy thought. She wasn't nearly experienced enough. Besides, with her on his back, his thoughts might not focus completely on the race. He'd be too busy concentrating on her sexy little body astride him. Either that, or he'd perform even better to please her.

Moor walked home, his stomach grumbling for a snack. All thoughts of food and flight vanished when he noticed a slip of parchment nailed to his door. It was a message from Jonis explaining that due to a family emergency in his home village, he'd be unable to train in the morning. Moor hoped the emergency wasn't too severe. Family problems were the worst kind.

As Moor stepped inside, he hoped for the best for Jonis's family. After eating some bread and two apples, he washed in the river then changed to Huform. He dressed, and headed back to the village square. Silently and without detection, he slipped through the longhouse and into Susana's room.

Smiling, he stood over the bed where she lay curled on her side, deeply asleep. She must have been more tired than she'd realized. Gods, she looked adorable lying there, her full lips slightly parted and her hair spread on the pillow like honey-colored silk. After undressing, he stretched out beside her, resisting the urge to tug her into his arms. Her soft, warm hand rested against his ribs. He covered it with his. His earlier arousal hadn't faded. The nearness of her curvaceous body stirred his cock. An erection the size of an ax handle did little to help him relax.

He must have drifted off, since it seemed like only a short time later he awoke to sunlight streaming in through the window across the room. The bed beside him was empty, except for a pressed flower resting on the pillow. He smiled, taking the flower as he walked to the window and gazed out at the village square. He'd slept past dawn, unusual for him. Though he hoped all had gone well for Jonis, he was glad his friend hadn't been expecting him for practice.

He growled, suddenly realizing his schedule was thrown off and he'd need to make up for lost time by training until late afternoon. After washing, he pulled on trousers and searched the village for Susana. He found her at the well.

"Good morning." She smiled.

He returned the gesture while longing to wrap her in his arms and search her mouth with his tongue. Part of their plan for secrecy was refraining from public displays of romantic affection, at least until after next week when they told Linn about their relationship. That was why he tried to enter her room late at night and leave for training before dawn.

"I won't be back until later this afternoon. I overslept."

"You must have stayed out late."

"I did. I need to stop at Jonis's before training to make sure everything's all right."

"I spoke with his wife this morning. She has a message for you. It's terrible about his brother dying."

So that was the emergency. "Did she say what happened?"

"Wagon accident. It seemed he and a friend were attacked by slavers"

Moor's brow furrowed. "Around here? Unusual."

"Jonis's wife said she heard from the local authorities that they seemed to be passing through on their way to the Vertue Mountains. It's terrible to think that slavers are still active."

"I remember years ago when I was in the Fighting Carriers, we chased off several bands from around these parts."

"Let's hope they're not coming back. It would be terrible if they started kidnapping people around here to sell as slaves."

"I doubt that will happen. There are villages without Fighting Carriers that would be easier to attack. I'm going over there and see if there's anything I can do."

"I'll see you at suppertime?"

He held her gaze, resisting another urge to kiss her. The sight and scent of her stirred him so much he marveled at his self-control. Tonight. They would have tonight.

"Suppertime," he stated before heading for the tack house.

After switching to his equine-half, Moor took his work saddle and weighted the storage compartments. Though he preferred training with a live rider on his back, the deadweight certainly functioned well enough.

Moments later, he'd landed at Jonis's farm. His rider had sent word that he needed to withdraw from the race. Handling his brother's affairs might take months, and he could no longer afford the time to train.

Jonis brother's village was a short flight away. Moor arrived in time for the burial and offered his condolences and assistance with any necessary work.

"Thank you, Moor, but there's really nothing you can do. I'm just going to make sure his family is settled and the farm is running smoothly. I'm sorry about the race."

"Don't be. I'll find another rider and maybe later in the year, if you're up to it, we can enter another one."

"That would be fine. Good luck."

"Take care."

Moor left for his practice flight wondering who his new rider would be. Inez would do it and he would take her gladly, but part of him still toyed with the fantasy of Susana joining him in the race. He knew it was impossible. Her job took most of her time. Still, he could dream...

* * * * *

Susana stepped out of the cottage and paused by the well in the village square. Sighing, she gazed at the moon and unbound her hair from where it was fastened at her nape. She rubbed her aching scalp.

"Hard day?"

Glancing over her shoulder, she smiled at Moor. The sight of him both comforted and excited her.

"Sort of."

He massaged her nape and whispered, "Relax."

She closed her eyes and leaned into him as he brushed aside her hair and kissed her neck. It was late and she doubted anyone was around, but he probably shouldn't be touching her so intimately in public. "What if someone sees us?"

"Why don't you come home with me where we don't have to worry about it?"

Susana's stomach fluttered. Spending the night at his cottage sounded wonderful. Her small room in the longhouse was rather cramped, and they needed to use discretion when he crept in and out, at least until she spoke with Linn.

"I need to eat first," she said. "I had several emergencies and haven't had a meal since this morning."

"I have food ready. I'm not the best cook in the village, but I don't think you'll find it inedible." He turned her so she faced him and caressed her cheek. "Would you like a ride? You look tired."

She shook her head. "It's a nice night for a walk. This afternoon the Chieftain told me he received a message from a new healer moving into the village."

"Is that good for you or bad?"

"Good, as long as she's competent. I love what I do, but if I have more help, that will mean I can spend more time with you."

"Ah." He smiled. "I like that thought. Now I almost wish I didn't enter the race. I still have to spend most of the next few months training. Speaking of that, I'm going to need to find another rider."

"Why?"

After hearing about Jonis's situation, Susana gazed at Moor with longing in her eyes. "I wish I was more experienced so I could ride you."

"I was thinking the same thing. The lack of experience doesn't bother me. You're accomplished in riding true-horses, and riding one of us is much easier than that. It's just that we'd need time to practice."

"Maybe when the healer comes, I can work something out with her."

He squeezed her hand. "Maybe. In the meantime, I can ask Dav or Inez if they'll ride me. I still think it's stupid to make riders mandatory in a race like this."

"It's such a long race, won't it be nice to have company?"

His brow furrowed. "Hadn't thought about it that way. Yes, I guess it will."

When they reached his cottage, Susana gazed around the large room while he brought food to the table. She'd been inside his home before with Inez, but only for brief moments. Now she took the time to really look around. His book collection amazed her. She had a library of her own, mostly containing books about healing and herbs, but his was filled with history and literature. Knowing the rugged, outdoorsy nature of Horsemen, she was surprised by his interest in a sedentary hobby like reading.

He placed a bowl of stew in front of her and she took an eager bite. "Not bad for a man."

"Whoever said men can't cook?"

"I don't know. I suppose it's the same as the idiotic idea that women shouldn't be anything except wives and mothers."

"Are those such bad things?"

"No, it's just—" She paused, a bit startled when he dragged her chair closer to his, took her face in his hands, and kissed her.

Susana closed her eyes, surrendering completely. Her fingers threaded through his hair. His lips were as soft as his body was hard. Each time he kissed her, it was like a fantasy come true. Everyday problems were forgotten as she surrendered to his tender lips and tongue. Warmth from his skin seeped into her, both comforting and arousing. Slowly, he broke the kiss.

"There's much to be said for being a wife and mother," she breathed, staring into his eyes. "As long as you have the right man."

"Do you have the right man?"

"I can't imagine any other." She clutched his nape and tugged him close for another kiss.

Closing her eyes, Susana waded in a warm sea of sensation. Moor's strong hands grasped her waist, dragging her onto his lap. She straddled him, her arms wrapped around his neck, her breasts pressed so close to his chest she felt his heartbeat thudding in time with hers.

His tongue gently parted her lips and hers met it with slow, tender strokes. Encompassed by his scent and touch, she moaned with pleasure. She drew a sharp breath when his hands slid up her ribs and traced the sides of her breasts. Plunging her tongue deeper into his mouth, she explored every moist corner and crevice.

Moor groaned with pleasure, his hard cock pressing through his trousers and her dress. Its firmness teased her clit. Her pulse racing, she rocked upon him, clinging with all her strength, scarcely able to breathe from the pleasure.

"Oh, Gods," she gasped, tearing her mouth from his and burying her face in his shoulder. Her cheek rested against the side of his neck, feeling his pulse throbbing beneath heated flesh.

Moor's arms tightened around her. His beard tickled her face as he continued kissing her cheek and temple. The man knew exactly how to touch her. She could scarcely believe all the years they'd wasted, settling for friendship when they could have been experiencing sheer bliss.

She paused, her entire body tense and on the verge of orgasm.

"Don't stop," he murmured in a husky whisper, his breath warm against her ear.

The sound of his passion-soaked voice pushed her over the edge. Her hips shifted as she rubbed her aching clit against his rock-hard cock. It didn't matter that they were both clothed. Sensations grabbed her in a relentless hold as she climaxed, panting his name.

Moments later, she sat languidly in his arms, a blush creeping into her cheeks. Didn't she have a bit of self-control?

He stroked her hair and moved slightly to kiss her cheek.

"What about you?" she asked, straightening her posture and gazing into his eyes.

He touched a finger to her lips, smiling slightly. "I'll collect after dinner."

Susana grinned as she reluctantly left his lap and returned to the meal. Actually, her stomach rumbled with hunger. It took only moments for her to finish the stew and take a second helping.

When they'd finished eating, they opted for a visit to Moor's private bathhouse behind his cottage. The village had two public bathhouses, one for men and one for women, but there was nothing more pleasurable in the middle of winter than a private room heated by a natural hot spring.

"I should have brought a change of clothes with me."

He tossed her a wolfish grin. "You won't need any clothes tonight."

"What about in the morning? I guess I'll just wake up early and return to my room."

"I can give you a ride. I'm up at dawn for training."

"I wish I could go with you," she said as they stepped, hand-in-hand, into the bathhouse.

"So do I."

He lit the torches at both ends of the pool while she closed the door. The pungent scent of smoke wafted through the room and drifted through an opening in the ceiling.

Susana shivered as she slipped off her cloak, kicked off her boots, and undressed. Gazing across the room, she noticed Moor watching her as he removed his clothes. She drew a deep breath, her belly fluttering as firelight danced across the broad expanse of his hair-covered chest. Gods, she couldn't wait to touch him.

She hurried into the hot water. Steam rose from the pool, creating a blanket of mist on the surface. Water lapped her skin and splashed against her lips. She licked away the droplets as Moor swam toward her. He tugged her against his chest.

Susana stood, her face tilted to meet his gaze. His callused palms, moist with spring water, caressed her upper arms. Splaying her hands across his chest, Susana glanced at the beautiful body she touched. Droplets of moisture glistened on the mat of hair covering hard muscle. The soft cushion seemed to swallow her fingers in places.

His arms wrapped around her, pressing her closer. Resting her cheek against his chest, she listened to the slow, powerful rhythm of his heart. Horsemen's hearts and lungs were much bigger and stronger than those of humans. Their bodies healed more quickly. Such physical power should have been intimidating, but instead Susan was excited by it.

She trembled with need just from touching him.

His lips grazed her forehead and temple before he kissed her full on the mouth. Before him, she never would have imagined profound communication occurring through a kiss. Of course lust and even affection could be expressed, but never the deepest aspect of love. It was as if words weren't needed. She felt how much he loved her. Through every movement of her lips, every tender stroke of her tongue, she tried telling him how much she loved him in return.

Susana's hands slid up his back. She grasped his shoulders, loving the firmness of his muscles. As a healer, she'd touched many people, both human and Horseman. Nothing compared to the lean, raw strength of the Carriers, especially the large ones like Moor. The ruggedness of his lifestyle was apparent in his powerful form and the sureness of his every movement. He could have crushed her with his strength, but instead he supported her with it. Gentle hands caressed her shoulders, arms, and back then cupped her buttocks.

His cock pressed against her belly. She reached between them and curled her fist around the stiff, velvet-skinned rod. Touching him thrilled her. Every part of his magnificent body aroused her in ways she never imagined.

His hand wrapped around her hair around his hand, holding it to her nape and gently tugging it backwards. He kissed her arched throat and stroked it with his tongue. Susana's eyes slipped shut as she surrendered to him completely.

Sliding down her body, he kissed between her breasts and licked both nipples. He kissed her belly, his beard scraping the tender flesh while he kneaded her buttocks and caressed her thighs.

"I love you so much, Moor," she gasped.

"I love you, too." He swept her into his arms and carried her to the edge of the pool. Leaning against the stone side, he guided her legs around his waist. She drew a deep breath of pleasure as his cock slid into her pussy. Still clutching her buttocks, he used his arms to rock her against him. It felt so wonderful, yet his movements were frustratingly slow. She wanted him fast and hard. Clinging to his neck and tightening her legs around his waist, she thrust her hips against him. The day's fatigue was forgotten as her body strove for a climax that hovered all too closely.

"Impatient?" He grinned, though desire blazed beneath the calm surface of his eyes.

"Very."

Suddenly, he pushed her away and stepped out of the pool.

"Where the hell are you going?" she demanded, shocked and irritated by his strange behavior.

Though he didn't reply in words, she watched as he withdrew a thick blanket from a trunk in a corner of the room and spread it on the ground. Taking another, he beckoned her with a look that aroused her even more. Shivering in the cold, she pulled herself out of the pool and approached. His hand closed around hers and he tugged her onto the blanket beside him, draping both of them with the other blanket. His body covered hers as he nudged her legs apart with his knee and entered her with a long, slow thrust. Susana clung to him, her fingers digging into his shoulders and back as he pumped into her in a fast, steady rhythm that soon had her panting on the verge of orgasm. What a fantastic lover he was. He knew exactly how to touch her, what made her writhe with passion. Beneath his relentless drive, she exploded, panting and writhing. His movements didn't cease, but seemed to grow in intensity.

Gasping, all Susana could do was cling to him, her eyes closed and head arched back against the blanket. His cock seemed to rub her in all the right places as another orgasm built, tightening her belly. Nothing existed except her and Moor. The rawness of his breath close to her ear, the heat of his body, and the scent of their mingled passions filled her entire being. Her heart pounded against her ribs while she held him so tightly her arms and legs ached.

"Moor, oh, Gods."

He kissed her to silence, his lips and tongue stroking and tasting. In spite of his kisses, she couldn't keep from gasping. He was claiming her body in a way she'd only dreamed of. All the power of an animal and the gentleness of a man merged into one magnificent creature.

She exploded, throbbing and shaking, yet he continued thrusting. His tongue traced the shape of her mouth while his hands grasped her wrists and pinned them to the sides of her head.

Yes, Moor, yes. I want to feel how powerful you are.

Forcing her eyes open, she met his fiery gaze. His face was tense, his lips slightly parted. His body had heated so much that she no longer felt cold at all, but warmed from head to foot.

"Let me touch you," she whispered.

He released her hands, his gaze holding hers as she stroked his face and throat. His pulse throbbed beneath her fingertips. The mat of chest hair rubbed against her nipples, arousing her further. One of his hands reached between them and fondled her clit as he pumped into her drenched pussy. The sensations were almost too great. Her clit was so sensitive that if he touched her any harder it would cross the line from pleasure to pain. He seemed to know this and used the perfect amount of pressure. She gasped sharply, closing her eyes as she neared another climax. When was he going to stop?

"This isn't…an…endurance race, you know," she panted.

He nuzzled her ear. "Complaining?"

"Not yet."

"Good."

His motions increased, pushing her over the edge again. Then his movements slowed, drawing out her orgasm to the final intense ripple. Withdrawing from her, he rolled her onto her stomach, wrapped an arm around her waist, and dragged her to her knees. He entered her from behind, filling her, taking her. Susana nearly melted into the blanket when his short, fast thrusts pounded into her. She leaned onto her forearms as he grasped her hips, his own moving with amazing precision that flung her headlong into another orgasm.

"Gods, that's enough," she moaned.

A rumble sounded from deep in his chest, whether it was a groan or a laugh, she couldn't decide, nor did she care as a final climax approached. Her tired body responded slowly this time, yet he didn't falter. As his breathing roughened and his big body trembled behind hers, she wondered if she'd reach that plateau that lingered just out of reach.

His fingers stroked her nipples, pinching gently. Susana moaned, nearly collapsing as she shook and reeled in orgasm. His hands returned to her hips, steadying himself as his entire body jerked. Panting her name in a voice raw with passion, he lunged into her writhing body. His cry of ultimate pleasure incited her passion again as he came, surging into her deeply. Rolling onto his back, he held her to his chest, his arms draping her languidly. Susana savored that perfect moment of silent communication when they spoke of their love through the mingling of their breath and the unified throbbing of their hearts.

His breathing returned to normal much quicker than hers.

"Ready for bed?" he asked.

"Uh-huh."

Dropping a kiss on top of her head, he stood and opened the door. She lay, pleasantly stunned, while he snuffed out the torches. Before she knew it, she found herself in his arms, her body snug in the blankets. He carried her across the snow to the cottage.

"What about our clothes?" she asked as he placed her on the bed.

"I'll go back for them. Keep the bed warm for me."

"I will."

She stood, shivering in the night's coolness, and rekindled the fire. Crawling back beneath the blankets, she stared at the door, longing for Moor even though he'd only been gone for a few moments. When he returned, she smiled as he lay beside her and drew her into his arms.

"Goodnight, love," he whispered in her ear.

"Goodnight, Moor."

Chapter Six
The New Rider

Susana's heart pounded with dread as she paced her room, pausing every few moments to stir the food cooking over the fire.

She thought waiting to tell Linn about her relationship with Moor would be better, but now that the moment had come, she felt like a terrible liar. Perhaps she should have been honest with him right away. No. It was better this way. Bursting into the Hall of Fighting Carriers with news of her engagement to another man would have been highly inappropriate. At least now they would have privacy.

Susana jumped at a knock on the door. Willing herself to remain calm, she greeted Linn.

He smiled and embraced her. She slipped her arms around him, his touch familiar yet no longer arousing. No man except Moor seemed to interest her.

"It's good to see you, Linn."

"You, too."

As they stepped apart, their gazes met. Could he sense what she was about to tell him? Impossible. Then why did he look so nervous?

"Come, sit down." Susana grasped his wrist and tugged him toward the table.

"So what have you been up do?" Linn asked, his tone rather stilted.

Susana raised an eyebrow as she dished food into bowls and brought them to the table. Usually Linn had no trouble keeping the conversation flowing with much more than small talk.

"I've been very busy. I'm glad a new healer will be moving to the village soon."

"Yes," Linn murmured. "I really need to talk to you about that."

Her brow furrowed. "What do you mean?"

"Susana," he stood, placing his hands on her shoulders, his expression pained. "I'm not exactly sure how to say this. I know it's something both of us feared from the first."

"What's wrong?" Now she felt worried. He looked so serious, so upset.

"Susana, about the new healer…"

"What is it? Is she a charlatan or something? Should I be worried?"

"No, she's an excellent healer."

"Really?" Though glad to know the healer was competent, she still felt a touch of curiosity, or was it envy? *Excellent.* The new healer was *excellent.*

"I can't do this anymore." Linn sighed, running a hand through his hair. "Susana, I've been sharing dreams with a woman. It's the new healer. I'm so sorry. I tried to stop it, but I couldn't help myself. I never imagined the dreams could be like this. Why are you laughing?"

Relief flooded her. She squeezed Linn's hand. "I've been dreading this, but I worried for nothing."

"What?" He stared at her, confused. "Did you hear what I told you? I'm sharing dreams with another woman."

"I heard. I've been sharing dreams with another Horseman."

Linn's brow furrowed and Susana's smile faded.

"Linn, what's wrong?"

"Nothing. Who is he?"

"You don't believe me, do you?"

"It just seems like such a coincidence."

Susana laughed again. "I should have expected this. You Horsemen are so full of yourselves. Yes, Linn, I really have a dream lover. Actually, this couldn't be more perfect. Do you think your healer would consider covering for me during the mornings for the next couple of months? I have the chance to ride in The King Montague's Flame, but I'll need to practice."

"The King Montague's Flame?" Linn looked even more confused. "Susana, you don't like flying."

"I do now."

"You really have a lover, then?"

"Yes, I do."

"That's wonderful. I'm sure Maria would be glad to cover mornings for you. I told her I'd talk to you about helping her establish herself in Hornview."

"Why don't you and your fiancée come for dinner tomorrow?"

"I think we can arrange that. By the way, what village is your Horseman from?"

"This one."

"Who?"

"Moor."

Linn's eyes widened in shock as he dropped back into his chair. "Moor? I never would have imagined."

"It came as a pleasant surprise to us, as well."

"So he's entered The King Montague's Flame, has he? He'll do well. Most Horsemen half his age don't have his flying power. As long as he out-stays his speedier rivals, he should at least show."

"Call me biased, but I believe he'll be fantastic."

"So you and Moor, eh?" Linn smiled. "When did this happen?"

"Let's not talk about when, it's just enough that it is."

He nodded, his smile fading slightly, as if sensing her implication that she'd been dreaming of Moor even when they'd been planning a possible relationship together. To keep their friendship intact, they directed the conversation toward other matters.

Susana sat across from Linn as they ate. Incredibly relieved, she was anxious to see Moor and tell him that she might, after all, be on his back for the race.

* * * * *

"This is so unbelievable." Linn smiled, slipping an arm around his petite redheaded fiancée.

Moor studied the couple from across the table in his cottage. For the first time since he and Susana had become lovers, he began to relax. Linn and Maria were obviously in love, which meant Susana truly belonged to him.

The night before, when she'd met the younger Horseman for dinner, keeping away from her room had been torture. Images of her wrapped naked in Linn's arms flooded his thoughts so much that he'd been unable to concentrate on reading, so he'd opted for a sprint and a short speed flight. No sooner had he returned from his cool down than Susana and Linn had knocked on his door. Guilt over his mistrust struck him when Linn congratulated them on their upcoming nuptials and announced his own engagement.

Even better, Maria had immediately agreed to take over most of the healing in Hornview for the next couple of months, so Susana could practice with Moor.

"What were the chances of both of us sharing dreams at the same time?" Linn grinned at Susana.

She returned his smile. Beneath the table, her hand strayed to Moor's thigh. "I guess it was just meant to be. Thank you again, Maria. I'm so looking forward to the race."

"It's a wonderful opportunity for me to make a name for myself in Hornview," Maria said. "I'm sure other healers wouldn't be as accommodating as you."

"I'm just glad I can be of help, and it will be better for both of us to share the workload."

"I agree. It must have been difficult for you being the only healer in the village for these past couple of years."

"Sometimes it isn't so bad, but other times I feel like I've gone days without sleeping."

"With both of us wanting to start families, it will be nice to have each other to depend on."

"Unless we end up pregnant at the same time."

Linn glanced at Moor and grinned. "Looks like they plan on keeping us busy."

Moor smiled slightly. While Susana could "keep him busy" any time she wanted, sex was something he'd rather perform in private than discuss at the dinner table.

"We really should be going." Linn stood, Maria's hand in his. "I have to fly her home and return to the Hall of Fighting Carriers."

"I'll be moved here by next week," Maria said, "so you'll be able to start your training."

"I can hardly wait." Susana gazed at Moor.

"Neither can I," he said as they walked their guests to the door.

Once Linn and Maria had gone, Moor tugged Susana into his arms and kissed her. While he enjoyed his guests' company, he'd been itching to be alone with his lover. For a while, he thought the dinner might never end.

She sighed, stroking his face and entwining her fingers in his hair.

"I can hardly wait until the race," she murmured against his lips.

"You're sure you're up to it? It's very demanding, not only for me, but for you as well. The flight won't be bad, but the land race can be tiring for a rider."

"Why is it everyone thinks healers are so weak and fragile? Didn't you hear me say I've gone days without rest? Do you have any idea how—"

His brow furrowed. "I never said you were weak, but this is different. It's very physical."

"I know it won't be easy," she admitted, "but I really want to share this with you, Moor. I don't want to hurt your chances of performing well, though. If you think I'll be a detriment—"

"No." He grasped her arms and kissed her. "I don't think that at all. I want you to ride me. I don't care if we come in dead last."

She laughed. "Yes, you do."

"All right. So I don't want to come in *dead* last."

"Just promise me if during the practice you feel I won't be a good enough rider, you'll tell me."

"Don't worry. This can be dangerous and I'm not about to risk your life if I feel you're not ready, but you're a good rider. As I said, the worst of it for you will be the land race. It's just the others we'll have to keep an eye on. Some of them race dirty. I've seen it happen."

"What do you mean?"

"Some Horsemen thinking knocking their competitors off-course is a good way to win, as long as no once notices. Physical attacks lead to disqualification."

"Physical attacks?"

"Don't worry. I won't let anything happen to you. I promise."

Suddenly she smiled, a wild look in her eyes. "Gods, this is so exciting. I wish we could fly right now."

He swept her into his arms and traced the shape of her lips with his tongue. "All you had to do was ask. Change your clothes and I'll meet you in front of the cottage."

"Ohh." She shivered with desire. "I can hardly wait."

"Me either." He nibbled her ear.

"Moor?"

"Uh-huh," he murmured, absorbed in licking her earlobe and kissing her neck.

"You need to put me down first."

Reluctantly, he set her on her feet. "Don't wear any underclothes."

"It's snowing outside."

"Believe me, you won't be cold."

* * * * *

As Moor stepped outside to change from Huform, Susana hurriedly undressed and donned the spare clothes she kept at Moor's, a heavy woolen dress perfect for winter traveling and a hooded cloak.

Outside, Susana paused, her pulse leaping as she admired Moor who stood on the snow-dusted walk. Though she no longer feared flying, at times she felt a twinge of nervousness before takeoff. Her anxiety diminished as she gazed at him, aroused by his beauty. His perfectly-proportioned body was in top racing condition. Just the thought of sitting astride his back and feeling his enormous muscles surge beneath her made her wet with desire.

He extended his hand to her. "Come."

She grasped it, allowing him to help her onto his back. Closing her eyes for a moment, she savored the sleekness of his coat as her legs slid over his back and her arms wrapped around his man-torso.

"Hold tight," he said and leapt forward in a tremendous stride that left her breathless.

She clung to him as he ascended fast, scarcely bothering to gallop first. His strides smoothed in midair and she relaxed a bit though kept a firm grip with her knees. Within moments, the wonderful, familiar sexual sensations flooded her body as he raced across the sky.

Her cheek and breasts flattened against his man-back. She uttered a soft murmur of pleasure as she listened to his breathing and heartbeat. Rubbing her aching clit against him, she mimicked the rhythm of his airborne gallop. Gods, it felt so good astride him.

Raising herself higher, she spoke into his ear, "Can you feel how wet I am?"

"Gods, yes." His deep voice rumbled through his back, vibrating through her woolen dress to her excited nipples. "Sit back."

She did as he asked, caressing his ribs as he slowed his pace. One of his hands reached behind him and raised her dress. Her shiver from the chill turned to one of lust when his fingers found her bare clit. Gently, he parted the soft folds of flesh and caressed the plump nubbin. Susana's heart raced. Filled with desire she uttered mindless groans as his thumb, drenched in her juices, rubbed her clit while his churning legs sent pulsations through her entire body.

"Oh, Moor," she moaned, certain her voice was lost on the wind.

"Yes, Susana, tell me how you feel. Talk to me, my love."

"It's unbelievable. I feel so…" She gasped, clutching his hard shoulder with one hand while her other slipped behind her, stroking his warm, smooth back. "I feel free but protected and so — Oh."

Words were forgotten. He rubbed faster and his pace increased slightly. Her fingers bit into his shoulder and equine rump as she leaned backward, lost in sensation. She just prayed when she came, she wouldn't fall off him. She needn't have worried. His other hand reached back and clasped her thigh just as she burst in an orgasm that nearly knocked her into unconsciousness. Magnificent pulsations rocked her from head to toe as his wings beat around her and cool air snapped across her upturned face.

His wings spread as he glided on the wind. Susana sat up, sighing with lazy fulfillment as she embraced his man-torso. "Sometimes I wish we could fly forever."

"So do I, my dearest." His hands covered hers, pressing them closer to his chest. "So do I."

* * * * *

Less than a week later, Susana clung to Moor as his legs and wings devoured the sky. They'd spent the early morning hours galloping over land and jumping fences and stone walls scattered across the countryside.

As they neared the Running Way at Hornview, Susana sighed with relief. Every muscle in her body ached. Moor was right. Preparing for the race would take some getting used to. She dreaded her afternoon rounds when she wanted nothing more than to soak in the bathhouse and relax.

Moor's flight slowed and he circled the Running Way before floating to a comfortable landing.

"You're all right?" He glanced at her over his shoulder as he walked to the perimeter.

"Fine," she said, relaxing in the saddle and loosening her grip on the harness swathed around his shoulders and chest. Slipping off her gloves, she rested a hand on his sweat-slicked back. His muscles rippled beneath his wet full-coat as she trailed her hand down his man-torso to his equine shoulder. She didn't doubt the saddle and damp blanket beneath felt uncomfortable.

Dismounting, she was about to unbuckle the girth when he grasped her hands and kissed the back of each.

"Go clean yourself up." He ran a fingertip down her pert nose. "I know you have to get to work. Once I take a breather, I'm going on another flight."

"I don't know how you do it sometimes." Susana gazed at him with admiration. "Now I know where that old saying 'strong as a Horseman' comes from."

He grinned. "Carriers are used to heavy exercise. I just want to make sure I'm fully prepared for the race. After all the comments about me being one of the oldest competitors, I want to make a halfway decent showing."

"I think I'm the only thing that will keep you from winning."

"You're doing fine."

"I feel like one big ache."

"You'll get used to it, love." He massaged her neck as she fell into step beside him.

Susana wasn't so sure about that. She needed to rub some ointment into her muscles, then maybe she'd feel normal again.

"If you don't want to do it, I'll understand. I know this isn't easy for you with your duties as a healer on top of training."

"I want to. It's the most exciting thing I've ever done. All my life I've been afraid of being daring. I've stuck to my studies and healing, but that's all."

"I think being a healer is one of the most risky professions of all."

She tilted her face up to his, wondering if her surprise shone in her eyes. She had no idea he felt that way. His career seemed so dangerous and exciting that she never guessed he considered healing risky. "You do?"

"People's lives are right in your hands. What could be more important?"

Susana smiled, warmed by pride. "Most people don't look at it that way."

"Most people don't look beyond the surface of anything."

"That's one of the things I've always admired about you, Moor, ever since you first came to Hornview. You're always willing to look inside people."

"Thank you." He stared intently into her eyes. "I can't wait until tonight, when we can be together again."

"Neither can I." It would feel so wonderful to be in his arms, warmed by the fire and the heat of his marvelous Horseman body. "I really need to go now. I'll have to relieve Maria soon."

He stopped, raising her hand to his lips. "I'd hug you, but I'm too sweaty."

Raising her eyes to heaven, she flung her arms around his waist and kissed his full-coated chest. "So what? I'm a mess, too. Be careful practicing this afternoon."

"I'm always careful."

She raised an eyebrow. "That's coming from the man who nearly bled to death after fighting an Ice Lizard a short time ago."

He grinned and shrugged. "The hazards of the job."

"I know." She gently slapped his beast rump before heading for the women's bathhouse. When she glanced at him over her shoulder, he waved at her. She smiled, giddy with love. To think, the man of her dreams had been so close and it had taken her this long to realize it.

Chapter Seven
The Competition

Four days before the King Montague's Flame, Susana and Moor arrived in Kingsville, accompanied by Inez and Terra.

"This is going to be a hell of a race," Terra said as he and Moor flew side by side, Inez and Susana on their respective backs. "I envy you competing in it."

"You've recovered well," Susana told Terra.

"I'm not in racing shape yet." Terra smiled. "Or Gathering condition, for that matter. I'll be ready for Gathering season, though. Then I'll think about entering some sprints in the spring."

Terra's speed was recognized worldwide. Many believed there wasn't a sprinter who could beat him, either on land or in the sky. He was faster than Moor, sure enough, though in a test of endurance, they would be close. Very close.

"You still have plenty of time for that." Inez slapped Terra's shoulder.

"How much farther is it?" Susana asked. "I want to get a look at our competition."

"Moor, I think you've created a monster." Inez grinned. "I can't believe Susana's the same woman who hated flying."

"That was before I knew how exciting it is," Susana said. "It's intoxicating, sitting astride all this power."

Moor warmed with pride at her words. He'd never lacked for admirers, but it was nice to know Susana found him desirable. "You can see Kingsville in the distance." He pointed to a cluster of buildings.

As they circled the Running Way, he recognized several of his competitors below. Some galloped for takeoff while others walked the perimeter, cooling down after practice flights. He'd arrived early and planned at least two more hard workouts on the course before resting a couple of days prior to the race. He shook his back leg a bit in annoyance. Though never fond of shoes, he had the blacksmith fit him with a set since he dared not risk an injury during the ground race. While shod, he couldn't switch to Huform. That bothered him more than anything, since he couldn't make love with Susana while wearing his beast-half. Once the race ended, he'd have much to make up for.

"Hey, that's Rex." Terra pointed to a tall, rugged-looking young Horseman with a blue-black coat and straight raven hair bound at his nape. His long, powerful legs swallowed the Running Way before he leapt into flight, spreading his ebony wings and soaring past Terra and Moor.

"He's one of the best," Terra said. "I saw him win several endurance races last year."

"He has a good chance of winning this one," Moor said. "There are a few others with good reputations. Marco from the tropics and Soloman from Sparrow Hill."

"Marco has a better record, but he's not accustomed to the cold weather up here," Terra said.

Conversation faded as the men floated to a landing and hurried off to the side, avoiding those galloping for takeoff.

Susana and Inez dismounted. While the men cooled down, the women volunteered to settle their belongings at the inn. They'd paid the innkeeper in advance, since most of the rooms would already be taken, due to the race.

"I'll meet you at the inn soon, love." Moor brushed a kiss across Susana's mouth. She ran her hand over his equine shoulder. As always, her slightest touch struck something deep inside him, stirring him, warming him.

Thinking how lucky he was, he gazed at her as she and Inez walked toward the inn.

* * * * *

"Moor should do really well," Inez said as she and Susana strolled across the village to the inn. "He's in terrific condition."

"He's trained hard," Susana said, admiration her voice. As a healer in a Gathering village, she understood the energy Horsemen expelled on flights. Until she actually began riding them, she'd never experienced it. Feeling the power of their bodies, the allegro rhythm of their hearts, and hearing the howl of the wind as they traveled was awe-inspiring.

"So have you," Inez said. "You've done wonderful."

"I just love being with him. I hope my lack of experience won't ruin the race."

"It shouldn't. Just stay on him and let him do his job."

"I will."

While Inez and Terra took a room on the inn's upper floor, Susana and Moor stayed in one of the more spacious ones on the bottom. The extra room would comfortably accommodate his beast-half. Already Susana missed sharing a bed with him, but it was only for a few days. Then he could eliminate the shoes and switch back to Huform. She had so many lovemaking plans for them after the race.

She'd just finished washing up and had changed into fresh clothes when Moor stepped into the room. Smiling, he tugged her into a rough embrace and kissed her.

"Were you able to see the other competitors?"

"Yes. Good looking bunch."

"Well, I have the best looking of them all."

"Nice to know you think so." He kissed her again, longer this time, his tongue stroking hers.

"Moor, don't," she breathed, entangling her fingers in his hair. "You'll make me want you right now and we can't."

"Maybe I can't, but you can. Take off your clothes."

"But—"

"Just do it."

Her belly tight with anticipation, Susana undressed and stretched out on the bed. Her gaze followed the movement of Moor's sleek, hard muscles beneath his brown coat as he approached the bed and sat beside it. What was he going to do? There was no way he could make love with her with his horse half.

"Isn't that position uncomfortable for you with your equine…form…" Susana's voice faded as his hands stroked her from breast to pelvis. He lowered his head, capturing one of her nipples between his lips. While his moist tongue flicked over the aroused little nub, his hand stroked her thighs, parting them gently. Drawing a sharp breath, Susana curled her toes against the mattress. He was going to pleasure her as promised. How decadent she felt, enjoying his arousing touches though he was unable to fulfill his needs. Covering her clit with his palm, he kneaded. One of his long fingers slipped inside her, stroking, gathering moisture that he used to circle her clit. Desire shot through her like a flaming arrow.

Susana sighed, clutching handfuls of his hair as his kisses rained down her stomach. When his lips covered her clit, she moaned, closing her eyes and arching her head into the pillow. The bed's scent was of fresh linen and Moor carried his aroma of leather and winter breeze, each scent arousing her along with his caresses. He knew exactly how to touch her. Using his tongue and lips, he lapped and tugged her flesh. She shivered at the divine feeling of his beard against her soft flesh. Susana writhed in pleasure, her body aflame.

"Oh, Moor," she panted. "Oh, Gods."

His touch was relentless. His tongue moved from her clit to her pussy, thrusting inside and exploring as far as it could reach, swirling, bestowing pleasurable torment. His strong, callused hands stroked her thighs and breasts. They warmed her belly and caressed the triangle of honey-colored hair between her legs.

Again, his mouth covered her clit, the tip of it running along the sides, the flat of it laving the moist little nub. His marvelous tongue didn't stop its rhythm until she exploded, her pulse racing and body writhing. Susana gave herself over to the wonderful, throbbing blackness. She'd become a creature of sensation alone, not caring about anything except the touch of his lips and tongue and the caress of his hands on her body.

She lay for several moments, her eyes closed, catching her breath. His hands remained on her body, stroking languidly, until she heard him stand, his shod hooves clinking on the floor.

Opening her eyes, a slow smile spread across her face as she gazed at him. His brown eyes glistened with longing yet held a touch of amusement. Everything about this man filled her with warmth and joy. Though his handsome looks aroused her, it was his spirit that touched her most. His inner strength combined with tenderness had grabbed hold of her from the first. She finally realized that dream sharing had only coaxed out the affection that had always existed between them. Smiling, she raised herself to her knees, slipping her arms around his waist and resting her head against his warm chest. His heart beat much more quickly than normal, further revealing his arousal. Susana stood on the bed, took his face in her hands and kissed him. Her fingers stroked his beard while she closed her eyes and enjoyed the sensation of his lips against hers. Slipping her tongue into his mouth, she tasted and explored every warm, moist corner and crevice. Her hands strayed to his chest. Gently, she pinched and teased his nipples. Thrusting her tongue deeper into his mouth, she caressed his torso. How she loved touching him. Part-animal, part-man, he was her deepest fantasy fulfilled. Stretching her arms low, she stroked the joining of his man-torso and equine-half—his Turning Point. Moor gasped, pulling her away, his breathing labored and his eyes glazed with passion.

"I need to go to the river," he said.

"The river? What for?"

"I need a swim."

"But it's the middle of winter. The water must be frigid."

"Good," Moor gasped as he stomped across the room. Before he left, she got a glimpse of an aroused Horseman out of Huform. Stunned, she settled back on the bed.

"Gods," she whispered to herself, "he makes a true-horse look deprived."

Still, the idea that she'd excited him enough to send him galloping to the lake thrilled her. Once the race was over and he was back in Huform, she planned on giving him a night he wouldn't soon forget.

* * * * *

At dawn, Moor and Susana walked onto the Running Way. Rex and his rider arrived about the same time, followed by a brown-haired Horseman with a chestnut coat. The chestnut was tall, rangy, and appeared very young. While Rex and his rider muttered to each other and glared at Moor, the chestnut approached. His rider, a young, brown-haired man, waved in greeting.

"Hi. I'm Marco." The youth extended his hand which Moor shook. "This is my rider, Jake."

"I'm Moor. This is Susana."

Jake's gaze swept Susana. "Pretty rider. So how did you get into a rough profession like this, honey?"

"Easy, when you're engaged to your Horseman," Susana said.

"Ah." Jake grinned.

Rex approached and said, "I'm guessing you're Moor, since I've heard Alexander is gray."

"Alexander?" Susana asked.

"There are only two mature Horsemen registered," Rex said. "Every now and then, it's nice to see older competitors in a race like this."

"Gives the rest of you hope for the future," Moor said. Susana nearly laughed at his sarcastic tone, but Rex didn't seem to notice.

"I think this will be a good race," Marco said. "I don't like this cold weather, though."

"It takes some getting used to," Rex admitted. "I like the west. Dry. Not too cold, not too hot."

"A Horseman needs to be rugged for consistent flying in the North," Susana said. "We're from a Gathering village and have seen so many come and go due to the weather conditions."

"So you're a Carrier?" Marco asked Moor.

"For about twenty-one years."

Marco's eyes widened. "Damn. That's longer than I've been alive."

"Impressive," Rex said. "I tried Carrying for a short time. Didn't pay as well as I'd heard."

"You need experience to earn good money," Moor told him. That Horseman needed a good kick in his hindquarters and Moor would love to give it to him.

Rex shrugged. "Racing's quicker, as long as you've got the speed and endurance for it."

"We better get going." Jake tightened his grip on Marco's harness. "Before the morning's gone."

Rex and Moor stepped aside as the chestnut galloped down the Running Way and ascended.

"Good luck on Friday. With all your experience, I bet you'll at least finish." Rex smirked at Moor as he dashed away, taking to the sky with a powerful leap.

"What a damn fool," Susana snarled, her body tensed astride him. Her rage seeped into him. Strangely, his anger dissipated. Knowing she felt so protective of him stirred his love. Rex and the others meant nothing. Only Susana mattered. He would race for her and for himself, anything else would be a waste of effort. "And he didn't look that young, himself. Not like Marco."

"That boy looks like he could hardly grow a beard," Moor admitted. "He had a nice takeoff, though."

"Rex looked like he was taking off for a speed race instead of endurance."

"If he can hold that speed over a distance, the rest of us are in trouble."

Susana uttered an annoyed sound and Moor smiled at her over his shoulder. "Forget about him. We have work to do."

"I hope he loses."

"Anything can happen during a race."

"I—forget it."

"What?" he asked.

"Nothing."

"Tell me."

"I was thinking it would be nice if you could beat him, but I don't want to put any pressure on you."

"Don't worry." He winked at her. "I was thinking the same thing."

Susana patted his arm before gripping his harness tightly as he galloped for takeoff.

* * * * *

Two days before the race, Moor had his last hard workout. Forty miles of ground travel interspersed with one hundred miles in flight.

They landed back in Kingsville in early afternoon. After he cooled down, Susana volunteered to give him a rubdown and grooming in the stable at the inn.

Moor closed his eyes with pleasure as her small, deft hands rubbed ointment into his legs. He resisted the urge to groan when she massaged his back and hindquarters.

"Gods, you have the most beautiful coat," she murmured, running her hands over his equine shoulders before sliding them up his man-torso.

Moor's eyes opened and gazed into hers. She stood on tiptoe as he bent to kiss her. His lips moved slowly against hers, his tongue slipping into her mouth and stroking tenderly. She felt so soft, so warm. Gods, how he missed making love with her. As soon as the race was over, the first thing he'd do would be change to Huform and fuck her until neither of them could walk.

"Seems there are benefits to being engaged to your rider."

Moor and Susana glanced sharply at Rex as he strode into the stable, his black coat lathered from his workout.

Taking Susana's hand, Moor cast Rex a warning look as they left.

"Typical racing trash," Moor said.

"I don't like him at all." Susana pressed her body close to his. "Want to take a nap before meeting Terra and Inez for supper?"

"Sounds good to me." He squeezed her affectionately as they headed to their room. "Three more days and we can share a bed again. Finally."

"I can hardly wait."

Chapter Eight
The King Montague's Flame

The morning of the race, Susana awoke at dawn to Moor gazing at her from across the room. Though he appeared calm, she sensed that his restlessness and excitement matched her own.

They exchanged smiles before she slipped out of bed and washed in the basin of water on the table.

"How do you feel?" she asked.

"Strong as a Highlander. I can't wait for the start."

"How long do we have?"

"Three hours. Ready to meet Inez and Terra for breakfast?"

"Just as soon as I braid my hair." Susana pulled on her clothes. She trembled and her belly fluttered so much she wondered how she could eat.

"Are you all right?" Moor placed a steady hand on her back.

"Just a little nervous."

"A little bit of nerves is good, but don't be afraid."

"I'm not."

He cupped her face in his hands and kissed her. "I'm so glad you'll be riding me."

Smiling, she hugged him hard. This was the most exciting day of her life. Soon she'd be astride him, galloping over snowy fields and soaring through the sky. She could almost smell the crisp air and hear the beating of his wings already. "I love you, Moor."

"I love you, too."

Over breakfast, Susana tried engaging in conversation, but her thoughts strayed to the race. Was she really capable of riding Moor without sacrificing his style? What about the rough play he'd told her about? Horsemen like Rex would probably do anything, dangerous or not, to secure a win. Moor was in no way an old man, but most of the competitors were much younger and at the peak of their stamina. But not their strength, she told herself. Most of them lacked the power of a Horseman with Moor's experience.

None of it mattered. She and Moor weren't really competing for the prize money, but for the pleasure of racing. It was a remarkable bonding experience for them, one they'd tell their children about.

"You all right?" Inez rested a hand on Susana's knee.

"I'm sorry. My mind's drifting."

"Don't worry about the race. Moor will keep you safe. He protected me for years during dangerous Gatherings. Other than Terra, I can think of no better Horseman to travel with."

"I just don't want to fail him."

"You won't. If he didn't think you were ready, he wouldn't allow you to fly with him. One thing about Moor, he's careful."

"I won't let anything happen to you," Moor whispered in her ear. "I promise."

"I don't know why I'm so nervous."

"It's natural," Inez said. "On my first Gathering, I was terrified, even though I'd flown before. A few minutes into the race and you'll be fine."

Susana nodded, forcing herself to remain calm. She was a healer, for goodness sake. Lives depended on her. If she could endure such responsibility, she could handle a race she and Moor had been training for.

* * * * *

In the tack house, Susana bandaged Moor's legs for added support during the race.

"All right?" she asked, running a hand over one of the bandages.

"Perfect." He grinned. "You apply bandages better than anyone I've ever met."

"Probably because I'm a healer." Though she tried sounding calm, her heart pounded wildly. In just moments, the race would start.

He dropped his saddle on his back. As Susana tightened the girth, Moor's family arrived to wish him well and await the finish.

"Good Luck, Uncle Moor," Silas said.

"Be careful," Lina told him.

"Beat the crap out of as many as you can," Pete murmured to Moor, hoping his son wouldn't hear.

Moor cocked an eyebrow. "I thought you said I was too old?"

"Like hell, though I wouldn't want to be you tomorrow morning when you feel every muscle in your body."

"I'm used to it. I'm a Carrier."

"Right enough. Good luck to you both."

"Thank you," Susana murmured, willing her hands not to tremble as she grasped Moor's harness and mounted.

"You'll be fine," Inez told her.

"Don't spend yourself too soon." Terra walked alongside Moor as he headed for the starting point. "I've seen Rex before. He usually blows his speed early, but saves a burst for the end. He'll be tough. Marco keeps a fast but steady pace, though I think the weather might ruin him. He's too accustomed to the tropics."

Moor nodded. "I'll keep that in mind."

"Be safe and good luck." Terra slapped his friend's shoulder before Moor broke into a canter, joining the others in a warm-up run around the field.

Most of the Horsemen and riders focused on themselves during the warm-up. Rex, however, cast Moor a condescending grin as they passed one another. Susana gritted her teeth. How she hated that Horseman. She hoped Moor left him in his dust.

The village Chieftain called for the competitors to line up. Twenty Horsemen had entered the most famous endurance race in the world. To most of them, the esteem of winning was worth as much, if not more, than the prize of five hundred gold pieces. Second and third place would receive three hundred silver pieces and a bronze cup respectively.

Susana tensed as she awaited the signal to go.

"Relax or you won't make it to the end," Moor told her.

"I am relaxed."

Glancing at her over his shoulder, he cocked an eyebrow. Suddenly all the tension truly left her. This was Moor, the Horseman she knew better than any other. What did she have to be afraid of?

No sooner had Moor turned his gaze back to the field than the Chieftain signaled for the race to begin.

Marco and Rex broke ahead of the others. Moor kept a middle pace with most of the runners while a few lingered behind, saving themselves for the final miles.

As Susana rose high on Moor's withers and pressed her body close to his man-torso, she forgot about the others. Only he existed, his powerful muscles churning beneath her, his wings pressed closed to his sides, brushing her legs as they soared through the first land portion of the race.

After a five mile run, the jumps began. Moor ran at a brisk yet even pace, nowhere near his fastest speed, but enough to keep the leaders in view. Marco, Rex, and four other Horsemen sped along at a sprint-like pace.

I doubt they'll be able to keep that up for the whole race.

Moor had explained the lead Horsemen's tactics, though. If they could put plenty of distance between themselves and the rest of the Horsemen, they might gain enough of a head start to win, even when they slowed toward the end.

Three quarters of the way through the first section, Moor's pulse sped beneath Susana's cheek pressed against his back. His coat dampened, his Horseman physique generating enough heat to keep her warm in spite of the light snow falling.

He increased his speed slightly when Marco and Rex almost disappeared on the horizon. Soon they were in view again.

"Doing all right?" Susana called to him.

"Fine," he replied, scarcely breathless.

She didn't speak again, allowing him to save his energy for the flight to come. By the time they reached the final jump, she was more than ready for the flight. Sticking to him on the ground was tiring, but in the air, her work decreased greatly.

The leaders had already taken to flight when Moor reached the takeoff point. A small group of humans and Horsemen were posted at different places along the route to ensure that no Horseman took a shortcut or used his wings for added power before the flight part of the race. Several of the judges huddled by fires at the shoreline, watching the racers begin their flight over the frigid northern sea.

Susana gripped the saddle hard, her hands tight on the harness as Moor ascended. Once airborne, she relaxed a bit.

Rather than keeping a moderate flight, he increased his speed until the leaders were close enough for Susana to see their churning hindquarters and pounding wings. Two of the four had dropped back, leaving Rex and Marco dueling for the lead before landing at the checkpoint.

Susana pressed close to Moor's sweat-drenched back. His breathing was harsher now, his heart a powerful, steady rhythm against her face. One of her hands strayed from the harness and slipped around his waist. She knew he was traveling faster than they had in practice, but that was a natural reaction to the race.

"Don't spend yourself too soon," she reminded him as a good partner should.

"I still have plenty more kick, love. Besides, we're halfway through the flight."

Susana couldn't resist smiling. They were performing wonderfully. In less than two hours, the race would be over. Though it was too early to tell for sure, she felt certain Moor would do well. Already one of the leaders had dropped behind him. Some of the rear runners had almost caught up to them, but he wouldn't let them pass. Only Marco, Rex, and a red-coated Horseman remained ahead.

The shoreline loomed in the distance. Judges awaited the competitors at the checkpoint. Tents had been set up for them to rest, have a light meal, and attend any injuries before the last two sections of the race.

"Hang on tight," Moor shouted to Susana.

She gripped him hard as he lurched forward in a burst of speed, overtaking the red-coated Horseman and racing wing to wing with Rex.

The younger Horseman and his rider shot Moor and Susana fierce looks as they leapt ahead. Susana's competitive nature, usually only reserved for her healing skills, reared at the sight of their rivals.

Moor followed, head to head with Rex. Neither caught Marco who had already descended.

Rex and Moor landed together, jogging off the temporary Running Way as other Horsemen drifted in.

Susana sat straighter as Moor trotted a short distance from the tent. She noted it took only a few moments for his heavy breathing to return to normal. Finally he stopped and she took the signal to dismount.

"You're all right?" she asked, her heart pounding with excitement.

"Fine."

"You did great." She couldn't help smiling as she took his hand and squeezed it. "Come on. You can unload the tack for a while and I'll rub you down."

"Sounds good."

"I'm hungry. How about you?"

He nodded. "I could eat, but I'm more thirsty than anything."

She didn't doubt him. His wet brown coat steamed in the cold northern air. Like the other Horsemen, he'd begun shivering almost as soon as he landed, the winter weather shocking their heated bodies once their flight ended.

Still, Moor allowed himself only a few sips of water before he removed his saddle, blanket, and harness, placing them under the watch of the judges as he cooled down. Too much water so quickly after heavy exercise caused excruciating pain.

Susana removed a cloak and blanket from his saddle bag. While he draped the cloak over his man-torso, she flung the blanket over his equine-half. Though she was no longer afraid of racing, her excitement hadn't ebbed. Sharing this experience with Moor touched and thrilled her. Nothing compared to this wonderful partnership they'd forged.

She fell into step beside him as he walked.

"You can go sit by the fire," he told her.

"I'd rather stay with you." She pressed close to his side.

Moor took her hand in his hair-covered one. Susana gazed at their entwined fingers and smiled.

Once Moor had cooled down, they walked to the tent where Susana unwrapped his legs and massaged ointment into every inch of him. How she loved touching him. Beneath her hands, his powerful muscles flexed then relaxed. A glance at his face revealed the intense pleasure he derived from her ministrations. One thing about Horsemen, they lived to be groomed.

When she'd finished, he offered her a much-appreciated neck-rub. His strong fingers massaged with just the right amount of pressure. Closing her eyes, Susana leaned closer to him and uttered a sigh of contentment.

"Feels good?" he whispered in her ear.

"Gods, yes."

When he'd finished the massage, they ate a light meal then rested for a short time.

Marco and Rex were the first to leave. Moor waited for them to gallop off before suggesting he and Susana begin the next leg of the race.

She helped him don his harness and saddle, using a dry blanket and storing his sweat-soaked one in the saddle pack.

Susana mounted and they galloped off for the last ground section. This would prove to be more difficult, as the terrain was rough and winding in places. The snow fell more heavily, making the ground slippery.

Moor kept a fast yet sensible pace, being careful as they completed the jumps.

Due to accidents and injury, it wasn't uncommon for some of the competitors to pull out of the race. Earlier, she'd seen a few riders fall during jumps, though a glance over her shoulder revealed they hadn't been badly injured.

This time, Moor had taken off early and was traveling fast, keeping a short distance behind the leaders. Susana had no way of knowing who was behind them.

Halfway through the land section, two other Horsemen galloped past Moor. They held the fast pace for several miles, then dropped back before Challenge Peak, the most dangerous and tiring part of the ground race.

The Horsemen had to gallop up a steep mountain with a narrow, icy path. A second mountain stood close to the first, leaving a slender but deadly drop to the ravine below. Should a Horseman slip, there wouldn't be enough room for him to spread his wings to fly to safety.

Susana and Moor reached the bottom of the mountain alone. Ahead, Marco and Rex battled for the lead.

"Crazy," Moor panted as he galloped steadily up the mountainside. "Dueling for speed on this path is suicidal."

"This mountain in general is suicidal." She noted the harshness of his breathing as he plowed up the steep, slippery peak. "Do you want me to get off and walk it?"

"No. I'm fine."

Susana didn't doubt he knew the limits of his body, but until they reached the top, she wouldn't relax. His heart pounded so hard through his back she felt as if it was in her own body. She wondered how he, Marco, and Rex could keep the pace.

The black and chestnut Horsemen were now close enough that Susana could see their sweat-soaked bodies struggling for the lead on the narrow ledge.

Suddenly Rex slipped, crashing into Marco. The black Horseman regained his footing and galloped onward, but to Susana's horror, Marco and his rider tumbled over the edge.

"Damn it," Moor grunted, quickening his pace.

"Gods." Susana felt sick with fear. There was no way they could have survived such a fall.

To her relief, when Moor reached the spot where the accident had taken place, Marco had somehow managed to grab hold of a thick root sticking out of the mountainside. Jake clung to his back, his face white with terror.

Susana and Moor glanced toward the top of the hill where Rex paused. For a moment, it seemed the black Horseman was going to help them, then he bolted to finish the race.

"Son-of-a-bitch," Moor grunted through clenched teeth.

"Help," Marco shouted to Moor. "I'm slipping."

"Don't panic," Moor ordered, reaching behind him for the rope in his saddle pack.

Susana jumped off Moor's back as he lowered the rope to Jake who wrapped it around Marco's belly and tied it as best he could.

"I can't hold on," Marco shouted, his expression frantic.

Susana stood, her heart pounding in fear, as Moor slowly backed up the icy mountainside, his hooves slipping. The weight of the other Horseman and rider would normally have been nothing to him, but the ice on such a steep surface made keeping a grip nearly impossible.

"They're almost there! " Susana called, glancing over the edge. "Just a little more."

Moor pulled. Susana reached for Jake's hand and hauled him up as Moor dragged Marco to safety.

"Are you hurt?" Susana asked them.

"Gods," Marco panted, trembling from head to foot. Jake sat beside him, gasping, as color returned to his face.

"I'm a healer." Susana knelt beside Jake.

"I think I'm all right," the rider said, but remained still as she examined him.

"My leg." Marco glanced at his right foreleg. "I think it's just a sprain."

Susana inspected it, agreeing that it appeared sprained. She wrapped the leg for Marco and told him to fly back to Kingsville as soon as he felt able.

The sound of hoof beats echoed below.

Marco turned to Moor. "Thank you for what you did."

"If you hadn't stopped, we'd be dead," Jake told him.

"Not a problem. This kind of race is about survival more than winning." His answer filled Susana with pride. Whether he won or not, to her he was the best.

"Speaking of winning, if you go now, you'll still have a chance," Marco said.

Moor glanced at Susana.

"Are you up to it?" she asked.

"More than ever."

Susana noted rage that matched hers burning in his eyes. How could Rex just knock two men over a cliff and gallop off?

Susana mounted. Moor broke into a run, his legs swallowing the mountainside, though he was careful to hug the inside and not risk injury to Susana or himself.

When they reached the top of the mountain, he leapt for takeoff. Rex's black form soared in the distance.

One hundred miles over the ocean back to Kingsville and the race would be over. A glance behind Susana revealed no other Horseman in sight.

"I don't care if you win," Susana called to Moor. "I'm so proud of you."

"You, too," he shouted, his wings pounding air.

Though Susana knew he longed to chase down the younger Horseman, his pace remained fast and steady, keeping Rex in sight. Just when Susana thought Rex might be able to sprint the entire race, his speed waned.

The grueling pace began telling on Moor as well. Keeping ahead of other competitors was difficult enough in shorter races, let alone one like The King Montague's Flame.

The race neared its end and the true test of heart began. Susana remained still in the saddle, keeping her body pressed to Moor's in a way she'd learned made his flight easier.

She no longer tried talking to him, since his breathing was labored. His muscles strained beneath her. Riding his sweat-drenched body was like being astride a lava stream. Rex's glistening black form loomed just ahead. His rider glanced over his shoulder, his expression concerned. He shouted something to Rex who stretched his legs and wings and soared faster, though a glance at his face told Susana the increase in speed was painful.

As the shoreline neared, Moor surprised Susana by quickening his pace. By the time they hovered over land, Moor and Rex flew side by side. It was only a few short miles to Kingsville.

Susana's heart pounded, not with the desire to win, but with the need to see the damn race over. The rescue on the mountainside had depleted energy Moor needed for the race. She didn't know how he'd managed to catch Rex.

Both Horsemen fought to keep their place, but the pace, particularly over the last few miles, had pushed both to their limits.

Susana tried ignoring Moor's ragged breathing and the way his heart pounded against her face. She tried blocking out the rush of wind as again he leapt forward, his wings pounding, keeping beat-for-beat, stride-for-stride with Rex. Through wind-blurred eyes, Susana could just about discern the crowd of onlookers gathered near the finish line.

Suddenly Rex soared ahead with a final burst of speed, passing Moor and gliding to the finish.

"I'm sorry," Moor gasped.

"For what? You were great." She kissed his nape, filled with elation. They'd finished the race and Moor had been fantastic. She doubted any woman could be prouder of her mate than she was at that moment.

Moor landed and trotted into the field, his breathing harsh as he slowed to a walk then stopped. Susana slipped off him, meeting his gaze. His eyes were bloodshot from flight. Distended veins created patterns beneath his sweat-drenched coat. His flanks and man-chest heaved, yet his legs were steady and his posture straight as he circled the field.

"I'm so proud of you." Susana hugged him before a small crowed formed around them.

"What a race," Terra said as he approached, smiling and offering to take Moor's tack. "Both you and Rex broke the fastest record in the Flame's history."

"You did wonderful, Moor." Inez kissed his cheek then hugged Susana. "And I knew you'd be fantastic."

Susana squeezed her friend hard. "Thanks, but Moor's the one who's fantastic."

"Good race," someone shouted. "We didn't expect you to give Rex a run for his money, old man."

"A run for..." Susana's rage bristled. "If Moor hadn't—"

"Susana." Moor grasped her arm, shaking his head.

"But you lost time when Marco—"

"I made a decision. I'm satisfied with second place."

Anger burned deep inside Susana. She clenched her fists and whispered, "But it's not fair."

"It's a race, love." He touched a fingertip to her chin and leaned forward, whispering in her ear, "We know what we did."

"If that's how you want it." She calmed a bit, though inwardly her anger still simmered. If Moor hadn't stopped to clean up Rex's mess, she had no doubt about who would have won.

Moor accepted congratulations from his family and several onlookers, then excused himself to cool down.

Others competitors started soaring in.

Only when Marco and Jake arrived and revealed what had happened on the mountain did questions arise about whether Rex would truly have won the race.

The prizes were distributed, but by Rex's expression and the reaction of the crowd, much of the glory had fallen from the winner.

"That was an excellent race," the Chieftain bellowed once the last prize had been awarded. "Rex had the fastest time in the Flame's history and Moor was a powerful and unexpected second place winner. Soloman followed up well in third. Hope to see you all next year."

"Yeah, then we'll see who'll really win," someone shouted.

"There's already talk of a rematch between Rex and Moor," the Chieftain announced. "What do you say?"

"I'm game," Rex said almost too quickly. The rust spot on his gleaming reputation obviously annoyed him.

Good.

"I'm sorry, but I'm not planning any future races." Moor slipped an arm around Susana. "My priority now is starting a family with my wife-to-be."

The crowd grumbled and Rex flashed him a scathing look.

"We hope you'll change your mind," said the Chieftain.

"I don't think so." Moor took Susana's hand, toting his winnings on his back, as they disappeared into the crowd.

"Rex isn't going to like not racing you again," Susana whispered. "He's not sure if he'd have won in a fair race any more than the onlookers are sure."

"Exactly how it should be." Moor smiled slightly as he held Susana's gaze. "Life's about choices. We both made ours at the ridge. I can live with second place, but a Horseman like that can't abide not knowing whether or not he's truly the best."

Susana grinned. "I never would have thought it, but you can be vengeful, Moor."

"Only when it's deserved. I could really use a nice long rest about now."

"How about switching to Huform and I'll give you a nice long massage?"

"You have no idea how good that sounds."

Susana ran her fingertips across his lean abdomen. "I guarantee it will feel as good as it sounds."

Chapter Nine
Just Married

Back in their room at the inn, Moor lifted the heavy bags of coin off his beast back and shoved them under the bed. He placed his tack aside and stretched. The numbness that encompassed him after the race had worn off, replaced by some muscle aches and a general feeling of fatigue. He was pleased with his performance and thoroughly proud of Susana. He hadn't the words to describe how wonderful it had felt to have her share the race so intimately. All that annoyed him was the potentially tragic accident. Though he tried disguising it, he was a little frustrated by Rex's win. Moor would have loved to beat the young snit. In spite of all his talk about how winning didn't matter, he'd tried his best—if just to steal an honor Rex didn't deserve after leaving two men to die. The race had been as difficult as Moor remembered. After helping Marco and Jake, he'd doubted his ability to catch the fast-flying Rex. Fueled by rage, he'd pushed himself to the utmost of his power, but during that final drive for the finish, he was too spent to match Rex's last burst of speed. Still, the doubt had been placed in the snit's mind as well as in the minds of the onlookers. By law, Rex had won the race, but everyone knew, had Moor not stopped, he might have overtaken the younger competitor. Not bad for— what had Rex called him?—a *mature* Horseman.

Quite honestly, second place sat well with Moor. After a long absence, he'd returned to racing with a very good performance and he had a second chance at love in the form of his beautiful, gutsy little healer. Yes, second pleased him very much.

It would feel good to finally switch to Huform and stretch out on the bed with Susana in his arms.

The local blacksmith had removed the damn shoes right after the race, though during the climb up Challenge Peak, Moor been glad for them.

"Let me have one more look at you." Susana stood beside him, running her hands over his hindquarters and stooping as she felt his legs for tender spots that would signal injury.

"I told you I'm fine."

"Humor me. Sometimes you can't tell right away if you did damage."

As her soft but strong hands ran down each of his legs, he grinned. When she touched him like that, humoring her was easy. Finally she stepped aside, but he tugged her into his arms.

"Thank you."

"My pleasure." She stood on tiptoe as he bent to kiss her.

While she undressed, he closed his eyes, concentrating on his Turning Point. With a shudder that shook the floor, he switched to Huform.

Naked, Susana approached. As he stroked her shoulders, her hands splayed across his chest. Holding her felt so good, especially now that their legs could entwine and, once rested, he could fill her soft, moist pussy with his cock and sate the desire he'd been holding at bay.

"Ready for that massage?" she asked.

* * * * *

Susana awaited his answer, her hands already aching to touch every inch of him.

"Oh yes. More than ready," he said in a husky voice.

"Good." She kissed the center of his chest. Her lips roamed over the hairy, rock-hard expanse. She gently nipped one of his nipples before shoving him toward the bed.

He stretched out on his stomach, his head resting on his folded arms. "You don't have to do this. You must be tired, too."

"Trust me. I want to." She knelt by his feet on the mattress and caressed his ankles and calves. His human feet were so well-formed, large with perfect arches. Her thumb ran along the sole. He twitched a bit and grunted with laughter. She smiled, loving how ticklish he was in certain places. Leaning forward, she ran her lips over the backs of his knees while her hands kneaded his thighs. The muscles were incredibly hard, the warm skin roughened by sparse, dark hair.

Lust twisted her belly, making her wet, as she rubbed every inch of his legs, buttocks, and hips. His Huform was male perfection with long, heavily-muscled legs and hard, prominent buttocks.

Finally she reached his Turning Point. It felt like a normal lower back, lean with sparse, downy hair dusting the flesh, but beneath the surface churned the most sensitive part of a Horseman.

Though he'd almost been lulled to sleep by her earlier ministrations, he groaned when her fingers and palms caressed his Turning Point. She bent and kissed his lower back, her tongue painting it with languid strokes.

Moor's reaction was volatile. His breathing deepened, his buttocks clenched. She knew by his scarcely restrained movements, he was willing himself not to writhe with pleasure.

Susana smiled. Gods, she loved arousing him.

"Don't move," she murmured, sensing he was about to jump up and pin her beneath him. The thought was enough to make her clit ache, but she had time to worry about her own pleasure. At that moment, she wanted to indulge him in every possible way. Riding him in The King Montague's Flame had been the most thrilling experience of her life. She wanted to show him just how much she appreciated it and how much she loved him.

Moor did as she asked, lying as still as possible while she continued kissing and licking his Turning Point. Her hands splayed across his lower back, her thumbs pressing the base of his spine.

Moor's control snapped. With a groan of pure lust, he turned, grasping her beneath the arms and thrusting her onto her back.

Susana gasped with pleasure as he kissed her breasts, his teeth and tongue teasing first one nipple then the other.

"I thought you were tired?" she panted.

"I got my second wind," he growled, kissing her belly and inner thighs.

Suddenly his mouth fastened on her clit. Susana uttered a sharp cry at the fierceness of his attack. His warm, wet tongue lapped and laved while his fingers explored her pussy. Susana's heart raced as she closed her eyes, lost in sensation.

"Moor," she panted. "I love you so much. Oh. Moor. Ah."

The tip of his tongue had found the most sensitive place on the side of her clit. The sensation was so painfully pleasurable that she could no longer stop the waves of orgasm from washing over her.

Moor covered her body with his and thrust his hard, velvet-skinned cock deep inside her throbbing pussy.

Susana wrapped her arms and legs around him, clinging so hard her limbs ached. *Yes, oh, yes. Nothing felt as good as being claimed by her Horseman.* His thrusts prolonged her orgasm and continued long after, driving her towards the edge again.

Above her own pleasure, Susana remembered that *she'd* wanted to please. Again, her hands strayed to his lower back. His flesh had heated, seeming to drench her with his energy and affection. Her fingertips pressed hard against his Turning Point, rubbing in deep circles.

"Gods, Susana," he panted, his entire body tensing. She sensed his attempt to hold back his thrusts, but her hands on the only other place as sensitive as his cock drove him to madness. His heart pounded against her. His neck arched back, the tendons taut.

She purred her encouragement as she continued rubbing. Her hips followed the natural rhythm of his as she gazed at him through half-closed eyes.

"Susana, slow down," he panted.

She did no such thing. The pads of her fingertips pressed harder, circling faster, as she thrust her pelvis against his.

"Susana." He forced his eyes open and stared into hers. Their usually calm depths looked wild and as desperate for release as she felt. His ragged breathing told her he was close. Briefly, she wondered if he could hold back long enough to carry her to climax.

As a healer, she knew the importance of a Horseman's Turning Point, but until she'd taken one as a lover, she'd never understood its true magic. Touching and stroking it in the right way gave her such power over this dominant creature. His incredible strength and stamina were literally at the mercy of her two small hands. That knowledge stirred her, thrilled her even more than the race.

The slightest bit more pressure on his lower back, five hard, fast thrusts, and it was over. It was enough. Susana exploded at almost the same moment Moor cried out in orgasm, his entire body rigid, every rock-hard muscle straining beneath slick, damp flesh.

He managed to move slightly to the side before collapsing, his body half draped over hers, his open lips so close to her neck that she felt their moist softness along with his warm breath fanning her skin.

Susana's heart seemed to take forever to slow. She lay still, utterly satisfied, a half smile on her lips.

After a moment, Moor moved off her completely, turning onto his side and cradling her against his chest. She knew by his deep, even breaths and slow heartbeat that he was nearly asleep. She was only half awake herself. The race had left them both tired. Lovemaking had soothed them enough for a pleasant nap before dinner.

Wiggling a bit closer, Susana sighed. For the first time in her life, she had everything she'd ever wanted.

* * * * *

"Let's get married." Susana paused in brushing her hair and gazed at Moor who sat on the edge of the bed, tugging on his boots. After a glorious two hour rest, it was time to meet the others for supper.

His gaze met hers. "I thought we were?"

"I mean tonight, instead of waiting until spring."

"Tonight?"

"Yes. Terra and Inez are here, so are your brother and his family."

"But I thought you wanted to plan the wedding?"

Susana placed the brush aside and sat near him, looping her arm through his. "I don't want to wait that long. Who cares about plans? Spontaneity is more fun. Unless you don't want to do it tonight. I understand—"

"The sooner the better." He smiled, pulling her onto his lap and nuzzling her neck. "We'll see if we can get an appointment to speak with the Chieftain and ask if he'll perform the ceremony. If not, we'll try one of the smaller villages on the outskirts."

After they'd finished dressing, Moor and Susana walked to the Chieftain's longhouse and were lucky to be awarded a meeting with him almost immediately. The Chieftain offered to perform a quick ceremony for them before supper.

It took them only moments to find Terra, Inez, and the others.

As Susana stood beside Moor while the Chieftain began reading the marriage rites, her heart pounded with excitement. Moor's gaze never left her. It thrilled her to see her love and excitement reflected in his large brown eyes.

"Congratulations." Inez embraced them as soon as the ceremony ended.

"I'm married." Susana smiled, the realization suddenly striking her.

"Luck to you both," Pete said.

Lina embraced Susana. "You have a good Horseman."

"Oh, I know." Susana slipped her arms around Moor's waist as he tugged her to his side. To her, no better Horseman existed.

The small group left the longhouse and walked through the village square, stopping at the inn for supper.

Throughout the meal, Susana and Moor could scarcely keep their eyes from one another. His scent and touch aroused her, yet even better was their solid affection and mutual understanding of each other. Those deeper emotions would last through difficult times and into their older years. Physical love was a wonder to be relished, but Susana knew in her heart that she and Moor shared something far deeper as well.

"When we get back to Hornview, the first thing we'll do is see the silversmith about wedding rings," Moor said. "What kind of jewel would you like?"

"Go for the diamond." Inez grinned.

"I think I'd rather have an emerald," Susana said.

Moor stroked the back of her hand gently, his gaze fixed on hers. "Then an emerald it will be."

* * * * *

A day later, Moor and Susana returned to Hornview. To repay Maria for covering her patients throughout training for The King Montague's Flame, Susana often worked long hours. Though Moor missed her company greatly, he used his free time to help Terra track down Kraig. Their obsession brought complaints from Inez and Susana, though both men were adamant about seeing that Kraig paid for his crimes.

Their efforts were postponed two months later when Gathering Season began. Moor was in charge of the village's first nighttime journey. He spent most of the afternoon checking gear and meeting with the Horsemen and Gatherers accompanying him. Susana was busy delivering a baby, but surprised him by arriving at the Running Way just before takeoff. Moor trotted to the perimeter to meet her, Jonis on his back.

"I wanted to wish you luck." She slipped her arms around Moor's waist. He held her tightly, her soft cheek pressed against his full-coated chest. Seeing her before the flight warmed him deep inside.

"Thank you." He kissed the top of her head. "How was the delivery?"

"Mother and child are fine."

"Good." He tilted her face upward, his thumb stroking her cheek. "Go home and get some rest. You've been up since midnight."

"I think I will get a few hours' sleep." She hugged him again and whispered, "I love you."

"I love you, too."

"Have a safe journey. Both of you." Susana glanced at Jonis.

The rider smiled and waved as Moor galloped down the Running Way. Once airborne, Moor glanced below. Susana stood watching the Gathering Party disappear in the clear nighttime sky.

Moor turned his attention ahead, pushing himself higher to avoid a strong undercurrent. That morning, Terra had led the first Gathering of the season and reported back that weather conditions were still more severe than usual in the Spikelands.

"It was a short winter," Jonis muttered, adjusting himself more comfortably on Moor's back as the wind grew colder.

"Very short."

"And Gathering Season always seems so long."

Moor grinned. He loved the challenge of Gatherings, and now that he and Susana had fallen in love, everything seemed to go by too quickly. Every moment as her husband was so wonderful, he never wanted it to end.

Just after landing in the Spikelands, however, he almost agreed with Jonis. In spite of their full-coats, the frigid wind sliced through the Horsemen's heated bodies. The ice seemed even thicker than usual as they chopped at it with metal tools to reach the Rock Blood. Though they'd waited nearly two weeks longer than last year before sending the first parties, the weather was still so severe that only a few Ice Lizards attacked — not that Moor complained about that. He and several Horsemen drove off the beasts before the Rock Blood was loaded into their saddle packs.

The journey home proved even worse since they hit a storm of sleet with winds so severe two of the smaller Horsemen were nearly blown into the ocean. Halfway home, Moor circled his entire party, ensuring no one was in distress, before he took the lead again.

"I think the Fighting Carriers should shoot the scout they sent out to see if the conditions were satisfactory for Gathering Season to start," Jonis shouted. He pressed close to Moor's torso to avoid the wind and ice slicing through the darkness.

"It's going to be one of those seasons in which we really earn our money," Moor panted, blinking his stinging eyes. "I can already tell."

His wings and legs cutting through the sky, Moor allowed himself a few brief moments to imagine curling up in bed with Susana in his arms. In just a few hours, he'd be there. In spite of difficult Gatherings such as this one, he wouldn't trade his life for any other. He had a fulfilling career and, more importantly, he had love.

* * * * *

Though Susana had always concerned herself with Horsemen and riders on Gatherings, it was the first time she'd been in love with one of them. She couldn't help feeling a bit overprotective of Moor, though she tried disguising it.

She'd been awakened shortly after midnight when one of the women in the village had begun a difficult labor that lasted until early evening. Thankfully, everything had turned out well. Afterward, Susana was so glad to have time to see Moor off before his first mission of the season.

She fell asleep almost as soon as she settled into the bed in her old room in the longhouse. When she awoke hours later, she guessed it was well past midnight. Moor's party should have returned hours ago. She'd left word at the tack house that she was spending the night in her old room, but there was no indication that he'd been in bed with her.

Worried, she washed in a basin of water by the bed and exchanged her nightgown for a shirt, trousers, and shoes. As she passed through the longhouse, several guards who had just left their shift were enjoying a quiet meal at the table.

"Has Moor's party returned yet?" she asked them.

"Not yet," one replied.

"Terra's group said the weather in the Spikelands was brutal this afternoon," said another. "So they might be later than usual."

Susana nodded, feeling even more concerned than before. What was wrong with her? She was a healer, trained to remain calm in all situations. It was perfectly reasonable that if the conditions were bad, gathering would take longer—especially if there were accidents, injuries, or illness.

As she stepped out of the longhouse, she was relieved to hear wings beating overhead. Gazing skyward she noticed several Horsemen heading for the Running Way. She hurried after them.

Moor and Jonis landed, both looking disheveled from flight. Moor was breathing heavily, his dark coat covered in frothy sweat. Jonis dismounted almost right away and the two headed for the supply house where they could relieve Moor of the Rock Blood loaded into his saddle packs.

Susana followed, keeping her distance so as not to interfere with his work. She should have known she couldn't hide from him. Glancing over his shoulder, he cast her an affectionate smile and paused, waiting for her to catch up.

"What are you still doing in the village?" He bent, gathering her into his embrace as she slipped her arms around his neck and kissed his cheek. Thank the Gods he was finally home. "I'm going to make you a mess. I'm drenched."

"I'm tough. I've ridden a racer, remember?" she teased, rubbing her face against his hairy one. He was right, though. Moisture from his full-coat seeped through her shirt. She tugged the front of it as she fell into step beside him and Jonis.

"That was a terrible journey," the rider said. "It felt like the Spikes had scarcely gone. We should have waited another week at least."

"Was it that bad?" Susana gazed into Moor's eyes, bloodshot from flight, and wondered if she appeared as concerned as she felt.

"We've flown through worse. On the other hand, we've certainly flown through better."

"That's an understatement," Jonis said. "Susana, do you want to inspect this Rock Blood now or in the morning?"

As the village's primary healer, it was part of Susana's duty to inspect each supply of Rock Blood for quality to ensure it would do its job and cure the plague.

"In the morning. I still want to get a few hours sleep, if I can."

"I'll tell the others," Jonis said as he took a sack from outside the house.

As Susana helped Moor unload, others from the Gathering began to arrive, all looking forward to a few hours sleep before beginning the day.

Susana waited as Moor returned his harness and saddle to the tack house. She fell into step beside him as he cooled down with a walk along the perimeter of the Running Way.

Susana ran her hand across his back and cast him a coquettish look through her lashes. "I'll rub you down before we go to bed."

"By the expression on your face, it doesn't look like we'll be sleeping right away."

"Sure you aren't too tired?"

He stopped, tugging her into his steely embrace and smacking her lips with a ticklish kiss that made her giggle. "Do I seem tired?"

"Not enough to miss out on," she leaned close and whispered in his ear, "having your balls sucked and your cock licked."

Just mentioning such things sent a stab of desire through her entire body, focusing mainly in her clit and pussy.

He drew a sharp breath, laughter rumbling in his chest. "Keep talking like that and I'll never cool down."

"Just keep walking." She grinned, slipping from his embrace and taking his hand as they left the Running Way and headed towards home.

Less than an hour later, after bathing in the lake, Moor stood behind their cottage and shifted out of his full-coat, leaving only his sleek equine-half for Susana to groom. While she brushed him, he rubbed ointment onto his torso.

When she'd finished, Susana dipped her fingers into the jar of ointment and splayed her hands across his chest, kneading the hard muscles beneath the mat of hair and warm skin. Gods, he felt so good. Hard, smooth, exuding so much power and sensuality.

"I want you so badly, Moor."

Wrapping an arm firmly around her waist, he bent and kissed her. Susana stood on tiptoe and slipped her arms around his neck, clinging tightly while his warm lips moved sensually against hers. His tongue slid into her mouth and she met it with hers. He knew just how to kiss her, how to use his tongue to tease and caress in a manner that sent her pulse racing. Susana wanted him to devour her, just as she wanted to pleasure him until he begged for mercy.

Reluctantly, he broke the kiss and held her at arms' length, his brown eyes gazing deeply into hers.

When he spoke, his voice was soft, scarcely a whisper. "Get in bed. I'll meet you there as soon as I shift to Huform."

Susana's belly tightened with anticipation as she brushed a hand across his stomach before walking toward the house. Glancing over her shoulder, she found him staring after her, his tail sweeping across his sleek, velvet brown hindquarters. His broad man-chest expanded as he drew a deep breath and moistened his lips with the tip of his tongue. Susana almost shivered with the thought of that tongue on her thighs or, even better, on her clit.

Turning, she practically ran to the house, ripped off her clothes, and slid into bed. Moments later, Moor stepped inside, his tall frame silhouetted by the moonlight shining through the open door. He closed the door and lit the two pillar candles on the mantle. Dim light flickered throughout the room and danced across his nude form as he approached the bed. Beneath his tanned flesh, his muscles flexed. His beautifully symmetrical body was enough to raise her temperature and flood her pussy with pure desire.

Susana opened her arms to him, a smile tugging at her lips. He slid into bed, his body covering hers, his lips buried in her neck.

"Gods, I love you so much, Susana." He lifted his head and gazed into her eyes.

"I can't believe all those years we wasted."

"Don't think of it that way." He kissed her brow. "Imagine the time we have now."

Slipping her arms around his neck, she pulled herself upward, flattening her breasts against his warm, hairy chest. His heat enveloped her, both comforting and arousing. One of his legs rested between hers and she wrapped both of hers around it, loving the sensation of how long and hard it felt—just like other parts of him.

His cock pressed against her clit and she ground her hips against his, enjoying the feeling of the hot, satin-skinned rod. Gods, how she wanted him deep inside her. Since grooming him outside, she'd been wet and oh-so-ready for him.

"Please, Moor," she panted, unable to control herself any longer. Her arms slid under his and she clutched his broad back. The muscles rippled beneath her hands as he shifted position.

His cockhead probed her pussy. Slowly, he pushed into her, a low groan of desire rumbling in his chest. Susana moaned, her eyes closed and her body wrapped tightly around his until he stopped, buried to the hilt, inside her. Instead of moving, he remained motionless, keeping her trapped in his embrace.

Susana pressed her cheek against his before licking his earlobe and whispering, "Tell me what it feels like inside me."

"Soft," he replied after a moment. Resting her head on the pillow, she gazed into his eyes as he continued. "Warm. Like the one perfect place where everything is pure, magnificent sensation and nothing could ever ruin it."

Susana didn't think it was possible to feel any warmer than she did, but somehow, he made it happen. "That's the most beautiful thing anyone's ever said to me."

Brushing his lips across her mouth and cheek, he moved in a slow, steady rhythm. He withdrew almost to the tip of his cock, then spiraled down in a motion that inflamed her desire. The urge to close her eyes was almost irresistible, yet she didn't want to miss the affection and desire burning in his expression.

"I love your eyes," she murmured through sips of air. Her back arched and her hips lifted to his. She took his face in her hands and stroked his bearded cheek and jaw, her gaze holding his. "They're the color of honey. So big and beautiful...oh. Oh, Gods."

His thrusting had increased and she could no longer keep her eyes open. Closing them tightly, she clung to him, enjoying every inch of his warm, hard cock as it drove in and out of her pussy. Her arms and legs clamped around him and his chest rumbled with a growl of laughter and a grunt of pure pleasure.

"Hold me harder."

She did as he asked, clinging to him with all her strength. Orgasm built deep inside her, tightening, pulsing.

"Oh, Moor. Don't stop, don't." She clutched his neck in a death grip while her legs locked around his, her heels sinking into his thighs.

She exploded, her vision black, her pulse pounding in her ears, and waves of pure pleasure crashing over her body. Susana lay, panting, on the verge of a deep and perfect sleep.

She moaned softly in protest when his cock slipped out of her. Gathering her in his arms, he curled on his side and stroked her hair.

"What about you?" she murmured, still unable to open her eyes. His hard cock pressed against her back, evidence of his unfulfilled desire.

"Another time."

"Not fair."

"It's all right." He kissed the top of her head. "You're tired. It was a long, long day for you."

"But I promised to give you something..."

"Don't worry. I'll remember to claim it."

"But..." Susana murmured, unable to finish her thought as the soft, silvery haze of sleep stole her consciousness.

Chapter Ten
Captured.
One Year Later

Moor's hooves danced anxiously over the cobbled walk as he paced outside Inez and Terra's cottage.

Beside dreaming about having a baby with Susana, he usually gave childbirth little thought, but at the end of the last Gathering Season, it had become very real.

Glancing anxiously at the cottage, he considered the events of the past year. After The King Montague's Flame, he and Susana had returned to Hornview. Between Gatherings, he'd expanded his cottage, including a herbarium for Susana. She was pleased to grow and store her herbs at home instead of traveling daily to the longhouse in the village square. The workshop also allowed her to treat patients in the home, something she appreciated now that she hoped to spend more time as a wife and mother.

With Maria in the village, Susana's workload had decreased. Moor was grateful for that. Though he admired Susana's abilities, there were times when he felt not exactly envious, but wishful that she belonged to him alone. Of course, he'd sensed that same feeling from her during the times when he was forced to cover several Gatherings in a day. After so many flights, he often wanted nothing more than to climb into bed, wrap his arms around her, and sleep. She never complained, however, and was always willing to provide rubdowns and massages. He knew how lucky he was to have her.

He couldn't have been happier in his marriage, and he liked to think Susana felt the same. As Gathering Season came to a close that year, Terra was called away to fill in for an injured Carrier in one of the tropical villages. Less than two weeks later, he and Inez returned with two important pieces of news. Kraig was finally dead. It seemed the vicious thief had quite by chance landed in the same village where Terra and Inez were working. Again, he'd nearly killed Inez, but this time he couldn't escape Terra's wrath. The black Fighting Carrier had rescued his wife and destroyed their nemesis in what Inez had described as an incredible midair battle. Moor didn't doubt for a second the danger and magnificence of such a fight. Horsemen rarely attacked one another in the air, but when they did, it almost always resulted in the death of one or both opponents.

The second piece of news was even more exciting than the first. Inez was due to deliver a child.

How quickly those months had passed.

Moor could scarcely believe he now awaited word from Susana who was busy inside the cottage delivering Inez's baby.

The door opened and Terra stepped out, looking uncharacteristically disheveled.

"How is she?" Moor asked.

"Susana said she's doing fine. Looks like hell to me." Terra looked concerned. "Gods, I'd hate to be a woman."

Moor's stomach tightened as he followed Terra around the side of the cottage where the tall, black-haired Horseman stood behind a bush to relieve himself. He prayed silently for the safety of Inez and the baby.

"Except to call for Susana, I haven't been out of that cottage since last night when her confinement started." Terra hitched up his trousers and hurried back to the house.

"How much longer do you think it will be?"

"Hell, how should I know? Do I look like a midwife? Susana said probably within the hour. I've flown some horrible missions in my time, Moor, but I've never been this anxious about anything in my life."

Moor smiled slightly. "What could be more important than the birth of your child?"

"Nothing. I—" Terra paused as Inez shouted for him. Without another word, he raced into the cottage, leaving Moor to his pacing.

Inside, Inez cried out sharply and bellowed, "Damn. Oh. If you try sleeping with me again, Terra, I swear to the Gods, I'll geld you."

Moor grimaced. It didn't sound too promising, though according to Susana it was pain talking. He wondered if he'd hear the same threat from her someday.

The shrill cry of an infant echoed through the cottage's open window. Moor quickly switched to Huform and tugged on a pair of trousers he'd taken with him. He resisted the urge to shout inside to find out if Inez was all right. It seemed like forever before Susana opened the door. He took her smile as a good sign.

She held out her hand to him. "Come in."

"Are they well?"

"Very well," Inez said as he stepped inside. She sat on the freshly made bed, her hair tied up and a smile on her lips. The baby squirmed in her arms. Terra sat on a chair beside her, unable to keep his eyes from his wife and child.

"It's a boy," Inez said. "We're calling him Canyon."

"A good name. It sounds strong and free, like a Horseman should be. Congratulations." Moor approached, gazing at the surprisingly plump face. "He's big."

"You're telling me." Inez raised her eyes to heaven then looked back at her son. "Doesn't he look like Terra?"

Susana slipped her arm through Moor's as they gazed at the new arrival.

"Yes," Susana said. "Through the mouth."

"Oh yes, I see it," Moor said. "But he has Inez's eyes."

"Would you like to hold him?" Inez offered the baby to Moor.

He felt a bit awkward at first but it took him only a minute to accustom himself to the warm little bundle. Suddenly he cocked an eyebrow and said, "I'm a grandsire."

"Yes, I guess you are." Inez laughed.

"Kind of a frightening thought, old man?" Susana teased.

He winked. "I'll show you how old I am tonight."

"Good. Maybe in a few months we'll have one of our own, then."

Moor smiled. The thought was quite appealing. He returned the child to Inez and kissed her forehead. "Get some rest."

"I will."

"Congratulations again, Terra." Moor clasped the Fighting Carrier's hand. "Once Canyon is old enough to change shape, he has a head start as a great Carrier, with your blood in his veins."

"Once Inez is up and around, we'll have to get together for supper," Terra told Susana and Moor as he walked them to the door. "Thank you for everything, Susana."

"It was my pleasure. You remember how to prepare the herbal tea I gave you in case Inez needs it for soreness?"

"Yes, I do. I'll take good care of her and Canyon."

As Moor and Susana walked hand-in-hand to the village, he asked, "You really want children?"

"Yes. Don't you?"

"Very much. I only hope we can. You know how difficult it is for Horsemen to procreate."

"Well," she grinned at him, "we can practice often."

"Very often." He swept her into his arms and kissed her.

* * * * *

Several months later, Gathering Season began. Terra had again been called way to the tropics. Inez decided to accompany him with Canyon, since Terra might be gone for several weeks. Without the Fighting Carrier, Moor's workload increased.

Though she never complained, he knew Susana missed him as much as he missed her. Between her work and his, they rarely saw one another. When Terra returned, things would get back to normal, at least until the end of the season push. Then he'd be swamped with extra flights to hoard as much Rock Blood as possible to last through the winter.

Just a little longer and Susana and I will have time together. It was a rare afternoon when he had no Gatherings scheduled. He'd hoped Susana could spare at least a few hours that day, but she was busy tending two men who had been involved in a logging accident.

After working around the cottage, he decided to take a short pleasure flight to visit his brother. He'd return in plenty of time to cook supper for Susana and perhaps give her a massage. Grinning at the thought, he galloped across the field behind the cottage.

Though the day was warm, a pleasant breeze fanned Moor as he spread his wings and ascended. Flying at his leisure felt wonderful. He soared, relaxed without the pressure of fighting the frigid Spikeland weather while carrying the burden of saddle packs filled with Rock Blood. Susana on his back would have made the flight perfect. He imagined her smooth legs against his sides and her soft breasts pressed against his man-back. Moisture from her pussy seeped into his back, stirring his cock and speeding his pulse as if he'd just flown fifty miles at top speed.

"Gods," he breathed, shaking his head. "I'd better think of something else."

An erection the size of a campfire log made flying rather difficult, and he certainly didn't want to show up at his brother's in such condition.

Pushing himself to greater speed forced him to concentrate solely on his flight. He reached his brother's farm panting, sweat-drenched, and thoroughly invigorated by the sprint.

Pete and Silas waved to him from where they plowed the field.

"Moor. Good to see you. How's the wife and that grandson of yours?" Pete grinned as Moor trotted toward him.

"Susana's busy but wonderful. I won't be seeing Canyon for a while, though. He's in the south with his parents."

"How are the Gatherings, Uncle Moor?" Silas asked.

"Going well." Moor ruffled Silas's hair. His gaze swept the field. "Looks like you've put in a good day's work."

"We're almost ready to turn in for supper," Pete said. "Want to join us?"

"Thanks, but I'm heading home. Susana will be waiting for me."

"We heard you've been pretty busy with Gatherings." Pete glanced over Moor from head to tail. "Must be true. You're getting ribby again."

Moor shrugged. "I drop a few pounds every year about this time. Too many flights, but you know the old Carrier saying, challenge is good for the soul."

"Hello." Lina stepped out of the house and crossed the field. "Supper's just about ready. Are you staying, Moor?"

"No, thank you. Just dropped in to say hello."

"How's Susa..." Lina's sentence trailed off as she and the others gazed skyward. The sound of beating wings combined with fierce shouts drew their attention to a group of six Horsemen, riders on their backs, ascending quickly. The Horsemen and humans wore leather and chainmail. Swords, bows, and arrows rested in their hands.

Moor's stomach clenched, his old Fighting Carrier instincts taking over.

"What the hell is this?" Pete growled, looking as worried as Moor felt. "Silas, go back to the house with your mother."

"Silas. Come here," Lina shouted, panic in her voice as she hurried towards her son who had unhitched himself from the plow. Before the boy could obey his parents, the Horsemen landed, surrounding him, Pete, and Moor.

"What do you want?" demanded Pete who had also unhitched himself from the plow.

"Silas," Lina shouted again. One of the Horsemen grasped her waist and hauled her to his chest.

"Get your hands off her," Pete roared, charging at the Horseman. Two of the others turned and kicked, their rear legs smashing Pete's equine ribs on both sides.

"Dad." Silas bolted towards Pete who staggered to his wife.

Another Horsemen belted Silas in the face. In spite of his youth, Silas's powerful Highlander physique served him well. The boy returned the punch, nearly knocking the older Horseman to his knees. Lina screamed, ramming her elbows into her captor's chest.

Another of the Horsemen approached Moor, his sword raised. To his attacker's surprise, Moor dodged his blow and disarmed him in seconds, slashing him across the chest. Blood sprayed the grass. The scent of anger and fear was thick on the air. If those bastards thought it would be easy to get the better of him, they were more stupid than they looked. Two others attacked. Moor's sword clashed with theirs as a third leapt at him from behind. He kicked backwards, knocking the Horseman onto his backside and sending his rider crashing to the ground.

Moor guessed they were slave traders, like the ones who had attacked Jonis's brother's wagon party last year. Vile creatures who had turned on their own kind, the slavers captured Horsemen and humans to sell or ship to the mines in the dreaded Vertue Mountains. Highlanders were particularly coveted, especially young ones like Silas whom they could mold into mindless slaves, digging and hauling in dank caverns until they died of disease and overwork.

Little did they know it would take more than six of them to capture a Carrier like Moor, accustomed to battling Ice Lizards in the Spikelands.

Within moments, he'd disarmed two of the Horsemen, killing one and wounding the other. His pulse racing with battle rage, Moor's powerful body responded with bursts of energy that easily outmatched his attackers. Pete had freed Lina from her captor but been struck a third time and lay bleeding on his side. Lina had been knocked unconscious on her way toward Silas who stumbled weakly, a dart protruding from his shoulder.. The boy's hazy, terrified gaze drifted toward Moor.

Nearly blinded by fury, Moor's rear hooves struck at the Horseman approaching him from behind. Only one remained a short distance away. As Moor charged toward him, his rider raised a blowpipe to his lips. A sharp pain ripped through Moor's chest. Glancing down, he tugged the dart protruding from his flesh.

Moor's vision blackened as strength flooded from his legs and he collapsed on the field.

* * * * *

Susana leapt out of her chair and rushed out the front door of the cottage. Her heart pounded as she gazed skyward, hoping the beating wings she heard belonged to her husband.

Disappointment tugged at her heart as she recognized one of the other Carriers flying overhead toward the village square.

Where was Moor? He hadn't been at the cottage when she arrived home earlier that evening. He'd promised to cook dinner and they had planned a romantic flight before making love. Already it was hours past suppertime. With each passing moment, Susana's worry grew. It wasn't like Moor to not keep his promises or to disappear without a word.

Overcome with concern, she smothered what was left of the fire and made her way to the village square. Perhaps one of the other Carriers would help her look for Moor. What if he'd gone on a pleasure flight and was hurt somewhere? Gods, why had she waited to long before searching? She wished Terra and Inez were still in Hornview.

Susana ran all the way to the village. She arrived at the square, panting and more concerned then ever. Two Carriers stood talking in front of the tack house. She quickly told them her problem and asked if one of them would give her a ride.

"Of course," said Bailey, a young man with a lithe gray beast-half. "Don't worry, though. I'm sure he's all right. You know how we Horsemen are, always flying longer than we realize."

"Not Moor," Susana said. "He's never done anything like this before."

"If you want, I'll take a look for him, too," said the other Horseman, a stout older fellow with a bay coat.

"Thank you so much," Susana told him.

"You ride south, Mac," Bailey told his companion. "Susana and I will go north."

"Good," Susana said as she followed Bailey inside the tack house where he donned his saddle and harness. "That way we can stop at his brother's, if it's not too much trouble? He might have visited there."

"Not a problem." Bailey stood still as Susana mounted. Outside, he galloped down the Running Way and took to the air.

It was the first time Susana had ever flown with anyone but Moor. Though Bailey traveled smoothly, it wasn't nearly as wonderful as flying with her husband. How she wished Moor was with her right now.

Halfway to Pete's farm, they noticed a true-horse and rider galloping at breakneck speed down the road to Hornview.

"Looks like a messenger," Bailey said. "Wonder what the hurry is."

"Stop and ask him." Fear clutched Susana's heart. A sick feeling settled in her gut. Somehow she knew the messenger was for her.

"Hey," Bailey shouted to the rider as he landed, galloping alongside him.

"Emergency," the rider bellowed.

Bailey sped in front of the horse and blocked the road.

The rider pulled up, glaring, as his mount stood, its sides heaving and coat lathered. "I have an urgent message for a healer called Susana."

"I'm Susana. Is it from my husband?"

"I'm sorry, ma'am. It's from his sister-in-law. Your husband has been abducted by slavers."

For a moment Susana was too stunned to speak.

"Where's her sister-in-law now?" Bailey asked.

"Gullville square. They had to take her husband there in a wagon to see the healer."

"A wagon." Susana's brow furrowed.

"His sides are smashed in. The slavers took the boy, too."

"Gods," Susana murmured.

"I'll take you to Gullville," Bailey told her.

"I'm glad I ran into you," the messenger said. "Otherwise that run to Hornview might have killed my horse."

"Cool him down good," Bailey called over his shoulder as he galloped for takeoff.

In less than half an hour, they arrived in Gullville. Since Pete was unconscious from the herbs the healer had given him, Lina informed Susana and Bailey about the attack at the farm.

"I hope they didn't kill Silas." Lina wiped tears from her cut and bruised face. The slavers had beaten her, breaking her leg while she was still unconscious. When she'd awakened, Pete was almost dead from his injuries. Silas and Moor were gone.

"No. A big boy like that they'll want to keep alive. He'll be a good worker," Bailey said. "I'm sure it's the same for Moor. They'll get what work they can out of them."

"You're sure it was slavers?" Susana asked.

Lina shook her head. "I'm not positive, but I don't know of any others who use those poison darts."

"We have to go to the Hall of Fighting Carriers," Susana said.

"We'll leave right now," Bailey told her.

"I need to send a message to Maria first, letting her know where we are, and also send one to Terra and Inez."

"Good idea," Bailey said.

Susana embraced Lina before she left. Though she trembled inside, she managed to sound calm as she said, "We'll find Silas and Moor."

"If I don't get my son back, I don't know what I'll do. When Pete woke up, he wanted to search. If the healer hadn't given him that potion, he'd be—"

"Flat on his back somewhere, considering the injuries he has," Susana told her. "Just make sure he rests."

As she and Moor left Gullville en route to the Hall of Fighting Carriers, Susana said a silent prayer for Silas and Moor's safety. *I'll find you, my love. I won't stop until you're home again.*

* * * * *

Moor awoke groaning, his entire body aching in places and stinging in others.

"Gods," he murmured, pushing himself to his badly scraped knees before he stood. Blinking bleary eyes, he gazed around the dim cave. The ceiling and walls were made of craggy rocks, the floor only slightly better. The entire place reeked of damp ground and old sweat. Several Horsemen stood nearby, staring at him, while others lay on their sides, apparently exhausted. All looked near starvation. Their human torsos and equine halves bore bruises, oozing sores, and old scars. Chains hung on their wings and wrists.

Noticing the chains on the others, Moor realized his own wings felt unusually heavy. He attempted to raise them, just to ensure they were still working, when a pain ripped through his testicles, nearly staggering him.

"What the hell…" He glanced over his shoulder, horrified that his wings and balls had been pierced with sharp metal rings attached to a short chain. Any attempt to spread his wings would result in ripped testicles.

"Welcome to the Vertue Mountains," said a deep voice to Moor's left.

He turned, his gaze sweeping one of the biggest Horsemen he'd ever seen. He had to be pure Highlander. His entire body, both human and equine, was made of solid muscle. Still, he was too thin for a Horseman of his size. His coat was dark brown beneath layers of dirt and scar tissue. If not for the filth matting his shaggy fetlocks, they would have been pure white. Moor guessed by looking at the Horseman's face he was much younger than his impressive physique led one to believe, no older than twenty-five or so.

"The Vertue Mountains?" Moor said. "That's where the slave mines are."

"That's where you are," said another Horseman, tough-looking, older, and with a scarred gray coat. "For as long as you last."

The cave fell silent as three armor-clad men bearing whips stepped inside, flanked by two tall, snarling Horsemen, also in armor and carrying swords.

"All right. Everybody get to work," bellowed one of the humans.

The slaves lined up, except for one who seemed to have trouble climbing to his feet. Moor could see why. One of his forelegs was swollen, perhaps sprained.

"Move, you hunk of horseshit," another slaver snapped, beating the injured Horseman with a whip.

Moor's teeth clenched and he took a step forward. A hand fell on his arm and he turned, looking into the eyes of a scrawny, red-haired slave who shook his head.

The injured Horseman had gotten into line and the beating stopped as Moor and the other slaves walked single-file out of the cave.

How the hell had this happened? Moor closed his eyes momentarily, imagining Susana. She must be so worried. And Silas. What happened to him?

"Where's the boy who was abducted with me?" Moor demanded of one of the sword-wielding Horsemen walking beside the slaves.

"Don't speak unless you're spoken to." The Horseman grabbed hold of the chain attached to Moor's balls and pulled. The metal rings cut into the still-raw flesh. Agony shot through him and he gritted his teeth to keep from crying out.

"I want to know where—"

The butt of a sword struck him hard across the flanks. "Close your mouth, you hunk of horseshit."

The corridor opened to a large cave where slaves, both human and Horseman, swung heavy chisels at the rock walls. Upon seeing reinforcements, they dropped their tools and stumbled out of the cave while the fresh workers picked them up.

"The boy you came in with was brought below," whispered the older, gray-coated Horseman as he passed by Moor. "He wasn't hurt. Now grab a pick and get to work before you get yourself killed."

"That boy is my nephew. I need to find him. I—"

"You." One of the slavers prodded Moor in the flank with his whip. "Come with me. We need a replacement messenger."

Moor followed the slaver, hoping to catch a glimpse of Silas along the way. He hated to think of his nephew alone in this pit. He prayed Pete and Lina were still alive and able to reach the village authorities. At least then they'd have a chance of being rescued. One way or the other, Moor would find a way to free his nephew and himself.

Susana, I love and miss you. I will find a way back to you. I won't imagine otherwise.

* * * * *

"I don't believe this, Linn," Susana roared as she marched out of the Hall of Fighting Carriers. Being a solely Horseman domain, the inhabitants walked naked through the halls and in the surrounding training fields. Clothes had been adopted out of respect for human sensibilities as well as for warmth while in Huform during the winter months. Normally the sight of so many nude Horseman warriors would have impressed her, but she was far too worried about Moor and far too furious with the Fighting Carriers.

After she and Linn had pleaded with their General Sota to send a rescue party after Moor and Silas, they had been badly disappointed. Since Moor had left the Fighting Carriers and there was also no proof that it was actually slavers who abducted him and his nephew, a troop would not be spared to search for them. If Moor's whereabouts was officially determined and slavers were involved, then Sota would send warriors.

Linn volunteered to locate Moor, but Sota was adamant that he remain at the Hall until a replacement instructor was found.

"It's because of the mark on his record when he left the Fighting Carriers," Linn said.

"I hate that General of yours," Susana snapped. "I know as soon as Inez and Terra get the message, they'll help me find Moor."

"I'll help you," Linn said. "I'm sure I can find a replacement by morning."

"Morning? Every hour could mean his and Silas's lives."

"Susana, we don't even know where they've been taken."

"The Vertue Mountains, where else would they take a young Highlander and a Horseman of Moor's physique?"

"You're probably right, but—"

"Thank you for your help, Linn. I understand you have your duty to perform."

Susana turned and continued out of the hall, rage boiling inside her. Gods, she'd never been so mad in her life.

"Susana, don't do anything until tomorrow," Linn shouted. "Susana."

She ignored him as she met Bailey who awaited her outside. The Carrier seemed as angry as she over General Sota's decision. He volunteered to take her as far as Diamond Plain, a hundred miles from the Vertue Mountains, but could go no farther due to his wife and children.

"I understand," Susana told him. "And thank you."

"It would be best if you wait for Terra and Inez, or Linn," Bailey suggested.

"It could take days for my message to reach Terra and Inez. I'll send them another telling them where I've gone and to catch up with me as soon as they can."

"You're taking a great risk going after them yourself. How do you plan on helping them without being taken as a slave?"

"I'm not sure yet, but I'll think of something. I have to find Moor and Silas."

"What if they're not in the mountains? They could be anywhere, Susana. Maybe even—"

"Don't say it. Moor is *not* dead."

Just as she felt the living presence of his love in her dreams, she would know if he was dead.

* * * * *

Moor tried picking his way down the stony path, doing his best to ignore the constant slap of the whip against his flanks. The slaver on his back was a lousy rider. At first, Moor had unloaded him several times in a row, but each time the rider had landed on the ground, Moor had been beaten by two of the

Horsemen. He would have fought back had another slaver not incapacitated him by using a hook on the end of a long metal pole to yank at his chain until Moor thought his balls might fall off. Finally, he allowed the rider to remain on his back. Anger simmering in his gut, he traveled the miles and miles of steep, winding tunnels running through the vast mine. His duty was to carry messages from slaver to slaver, or to haul lighter loads of precious gems to the mine's entrance. The work itself wouldn't have been bad, if he was shod. The sharp stones littering the trails tore at his hooves, particularly when the rider demanded speed. He noticed other Horsemen, messengers like himself, stumbling along on broken hooves, some worn to the nub and dripping blood. Gods, how he hated the slavers.

With all the traveling he did as a messenger, he expected to see Silas somewhere, but it had been over a week and there had been no sign of his nephew. The gray-coated Horseman had said a boy had been brought in with Moor, but what if it hadn't been Silas? What if he had been sent somewhere else, or worse, had been killed?

Suddenly, one of Moor's front hooves turned in a hole.

"Clumsy bastard," his rider growled.

Moor's heart pounded. A little harder and his leg might have snapped. Already soreness had begun seeping into his legs, though it was more from the trail's condition than from the traveling itself.

"If you knew how to ride instead of sitting there like a sack of bricks, it would be easier on both of us," Moor snarled.

The butt of the whip slammed between his man-shoulders. Moor grunted, itching to strangle the slaver, but his hands were manacled in front of him—a precaution they'd taken because of all the fights he'd put up.

"You're not here for an easy life. You're here to work."

"Hey." Another Horseman, tall, dark-haired, his torso covered in black leather armor, approached. Moor knew him to be one of the leaders. "How's that Horseman working out?"

"Other than having a sharp mouth, he's strong as ten oxen," Moor's rider said. "He runs these tunnels all day and most of the night and I don't think he's even broken a sweat."

Moor bit back a reply. Since arriving in the mine, scarcely an hour went by when he wasn't dripping wet from heat and heavy labor. The way he and the others were tied up didn't allow for proper care of their skin and coats, and Moor's felt so grubby he'd need a saw to scrape off the filth. His muscles ached from constant work without proper cool downs and grooming. With the chains attached to his wings and testicles, he was unable to switch to Huform, since there was no way of knowing where the metal hooks piercing his flesh would end up. They could cause serious internal damage when he shifted shape. The chains were the only means the slavers had of keeping control of the Horsemen. Otherwise, they would fight for their lives and fly away.

Any length of time spent in this place, and Moor knew he'd be wrecked, just as so many of the Horsemen around him were injured beyond repair. He longed to be back in his cottage, Susana snug in his arms. Those sweet moments spent with her seemed so far away.

"He's got more stamina than all our best messengers put together," the rider continued.

"Good. One of the pullers below croaked this morning. We need a replacement. If he's as strong as you say, he'll do well, even if he's not as big as most of the other Highlanders down there."

For the first time in his life, Moor was sorry for the Highlander blood in his background.

"Damn it," the rider grumbled, slapping Moor's hindquarters with the whip. "I was getting used to him."

"If most of the loads get cleared away this week, you can have him back."

As Moor followed the Horseman slaver deeper into the mine, he stared at each worker he passed, hoping to catch a glimpse of Silas. The lower they headed, the heavier the air became, thick with smoke from torches that provided the only light in the caves. The creak of wagon wheels, the echo of picks striking rock, and the coughs and groans of sick, overworked slaves filled the corridors.

The slaver used the butt of his whip to nudge Moor into a vast cave where several human workers chiseled the walls while three Highlanders hauled huge wagonloads of rock. Moor immediately recognized the enormous Highlander who'd spoken to him upon his arrival in the mines.

"Hitch up over there." The slaver pointed to a wagon filled with rocks in a corner of the cave. Moor did as he was told, falling into step behind the other pullers as they left the chamber and headed for another cave where the rocks were piled. At least his manacles had been removed before he started pulling.

As he worked, he noted none of the slavers remained behind to supervise.

"There are no overseers here," Moor commented. "It seems strange that—"

"Don't even think about not working or trying to escape," said the Horseman pulling just behind him. "They inspect every hour or so, and if the work's not done, they beat the shit out of all of us."

"It would be hard to beat all of us if we tried fighting our way out of here."

"Don't even think about it," the enormous Highlander glared over his shoulder at Moor. "There are more slavers here than you think, and even if we did escape, the mountains are loaded with Stonesnakes."

Moor had heard of Stonesnakes. Nearly as large as Ice Lizards, they could squeeze the life out of a full-grown Horseman—even one of the enormous Highlander's proportions.

"I think I'd rather take my chances with the Stonesnakes," Moor said. "At least they kill fast, not slow like these damn slavers."

The huge Highlander snarled, his dark eyes blazing. "Do I look like a weasel to you? Do the rest of us? Trust me when I say there is no escaping from here. I've tried and failed, and I'm not the only one."

"I'm not about to give up and fall in line," Moor said. "I have a wife, a—"

"We all had families once," snapped a puller from the back of the line. "You'll do best to forget everyone and everything from your old life."

Moor wasn't sure if he felt more enraged or disgusted. How could these people just give up like this?

"Don't get any ideas about making trouble here," said the Horseman behind Moor. "Slavers aren't the only ones who get violent when the rules are broken. Our lives are bad enough without some new hero coming in here making things worse."

"If you can fight me, you can fight them," Moor said.

"There's only one of you. Remember that."

Moor glared at the man.

"Obey. It will be easiest for you," said the largest Highlander. Strangely, his voice and expression held not a hint of threat, only quiet resignation. "There's no point in fighting each other."

Moor had to agree there. The big one seemed the most approachable, so he asked, "Have you seen a boy named Silas? He's my nephew. We were abducted at the same time."

No one responded. Moor sighed, leaning into the harness wrapped around his man-torso and beast belly. It was really too big for him, and he knew after so many hours, his skin would be rubbed raw.

As the others had warned, the slavers checked their progress every hour. Anyone, human or Horseman, who didn't appear to be working to the fullest of his potential, was lashed and sent back to mining without so much as water to tend his broken skin.

To Moor, the hours dragged by with agonizing slowness. As he'd predicted, the ill-fitting harness rubbed his skin raw in places. Though large for a Carrier, he didn't have the pulling capacity of a full Highlander. By the time the next shift relieved them for the night, he felt almost too exhausted to move. Every muscle in his body burned. His hooves ached from the jagged pathways and he missed Susana more than ever.

"You'll get used to the loads."

Moor glanced at the enormous Highlander who had fallen into step beside him. He noted the Horseman's heavily muscled torso and equine back also bore a few open sores from his harness, though a buildup of scar tissue prevented the oozing rawness noticeable on Moor's flesh.

"You're strong for your size," the younger man continued.

Moor's lips twisted in a wry grin. He certainly didn't feel strong, but he knew it was quite a compliment from such a powerful Highlander. "I don't think I've ever seen any Horseman pull as much as you do."

The youth's chin lifted and he squared his massive shoulders. "There's nothing these slavers can give me that I can't pull. It's one way they'll never beat me."

"What's your name?" Moor asked.

The man's expression hardened. "We don't have names here."

"I'm Moor."

"I said we don't have names here."

They plodded up the pathway to the sleeping quarters where several Horsemen and humans already slumbered on the hard ground. While many of the Horsemen were tired enough to lie down, others, like Moor's burly companion, slept standing up.

Though he hated lying down in his equine form, Moor decided he was exhausted enough to do just that. Dropping onto his side, he stared at the torchlight dancing on the rock wall.

The big Highlander stood beside him. Moor was nearly asleep when the young man whispered, "I've seen your nephew."

"Silas?" Moor snapped awake.

"Yes. He's pulling in one of the upper caves. I was with him the first few days. He had some trouble getting adjusted, but he's all right. I told him to do what the slavers want him to and he'll be fine. He's a strong boy."

"Thank you."

Sadness flashed across the Highlander's stony features. "I know what he's going through. I was even younger than him when I came here."

"How long have you been here?"

The Highlander shrugged. "I lost count a long time ago."

"Why don't any of you—"

"Enough talk. We have little time to rest as it is." He strode away from Moor, surprisingly smooth-gaited for a creature of his size. If the youth had a chance to get out of these mines, Moor had an inkling a Horseman of such quality could go far. Unfortunately, slavery seemed to have stolen even the smallest particle of hope from these men.

Moor was too tired to think anymore. Allowing the image of Susana to fill his mind, he drifted to sleep...and was awakened what seemed like moments later by a hard kick in the hindquarters.

His eyes opened in time for him to roll out of the way of another kick aimed at his face. As he struggled to his feet, yet another set of hooves struck him in the side. Moor grunted, raising his arms to block a barrage of kicks. He tasted blood and his vision blackened. Fury and fear pushed him to his feet. Striking out with his rear hooves, he knocked one of his attackers into the cave wall. Leaping aside, he avoided a fist in the face and snapped out with his own, staggering another slave whom he recognized as the Horseman who'd pulled the wagon behind him earlier that day.

"Enough," bellowed a deep voice. The largest Highlander shoved his way past the kicking, punching Horsemen.

The group circled Moor, but didn't attack.

"He's a troublemaker," snapped one of the Horsemen Moor had punched. He wiped blood from his lips.

"Someone like him can make life hard for the rest of us," said another.

"I said that's enough," the tall youth repeated, his gaze sweeping the men.

"He's new," said the older, gray-coated slave who had spoken to Moor on the day of his arrival. "He'll grow accustomed to the mines soon enough, but if you ask me, it's nice to see a Horseman who hasn't yet lost his spirit."

"Hard to keep your spirit in this place," someone muttered as the group dispersed.

Moor wiped blood from a gash above his eye and pressed a hand to his bruised chest. He glanced at his two defenders. "Thank you."

"You can thank us by keeping your mouth shut and doing what you're told," said the youth.

"I've never been good at that."

"You better learn." The young Horseman's expression hardened as he walked away.

"He's right," the gray-coated one said. "I was like you once and he...he was even worse. We both learned the hard way that escape is impossible."

"I have to find a way out. My wife—"

"Forget her."

Moor's fists clenched and his pulse raced. *Forget Susana.* "I can't do that."

"Then your life will be even more miserable than it has to be." The older Horseman walked away, leaving Moor to spend the rest of the night in thought, since he didn't dare risk sleeping again.

* * * * *

Over the next couple of weeks, Moor continued pulling heavy loads in the mine's lowest levels. Only the strongest workers with the best stamina were sent there, and though they worked hard, he also noticed they were the only Horsemen who received enough food and water to really keep their strength up. Still, it wasn't nearly enough to satisfy. He always felt hungry and thirsty. Though he grew accustomed to pulling, his body always ached from head to tail by the time he retired to sleep.

The other slaves spoke little to one another and even less to Moor. No one ever called anyone else by name. The only one who gave him a decent word was the older, gray-coated Horseman. This man seemed to be a close friend of the powerful Highlander. The youth looked on him almost as a father-figure, strange, since the other slaves appeared to treat the young man as a leader. If there were arguments, he settled them. If the guards left work to be split among a group, the slaves always looked to the Highlander to take charge. Not only did the boy have tremendous size and strength in his favor, but he had a calm, fair temperament. In spite of his apparent acceptance of his life, Moor saw anger deep in the young Horseman's eyes — and desire. Desire to be free of his bonds and the mines.

If Moor could only come up with a plan to escape then convince the Highlander to rally they others... No. It wouldn't work. They'd all made that clear enough. What were they afraid of? Surely even death was better than this slavery.

Chapter Eleven
The Healer

Moor closed his eyes for a moment and rolled his shoulders as he dropped his harness on the cave floor.

He stepped aside as the replacement slave approached the wagon and took up the harness. Normally, he'd have looked forward to a few hours of sleep on the hard, rocky ground, but today he was allowed to bathe. The guards rarely allowed the slaves in the spring, and they were never given enough time to truly enjoy the cool water that flowed through one of the caves on the upper level.

Other than missing Susana, Inez, and Hornview itself, the lack of washing bothered Moor most. He couldn't seem to accustom himself to the stench of stinking bodies, his own seeming the worst. Probably because his skin and coat felt so cruddy from dirt and sore from the constant rubbing of the harness. If he remained in the mine long enough, the scars would probably be permanent. Switching between Huform and equine-half sped Horsemen's healing process and even helped them recover from diseases faster than humans. Because of the chains, it had been so long since Moor had switched to Huform that he wondered if he'd remember how. He didn't doubt it would be extremely uncomfortable. Unless Horsemen took proper care of their skin, coats, and muscles, changing shape was painful. The mine would destroy him and the others. He had to find a way out.

"Get up, you sack of horseshit," growled one of the guards, lashing his whip across the flanks of a slave who'd stumbled to his knees before reaching his wagon. The slave coughed deep and hard, unable to catch his breath. One look in his feverish eyes, and Moor knew he was very ill.

Approaching, he offered the slave a hand up, only to feel the cut of a whip across his back.

"Your shift is over. Get the hell out of here and to the baths, you stinking Horseman," roared the guard.

"He's sick." Moor glared.

"Nobody misses a shift."

"If you let him rest, then he'll recover and can do a decent day's work again."

"He'll work until he croaks, like the rest of you stinking animals."

Moor's gut burned with hatred. "Wouldn't it be more profitable to allow him to recover instead of going through the trouble of replacing him with another slave, should he die?"

"You're not here to think, you sack of horseshit."

"Wait a minute. He might have a point." The guard standing in the doorway stepped forward, a wicked grin on his lips. He stared hard at Moor. "You think you're so smart. You want to work his shift instead of washing and sleeping? Doesn't sound like such a good idea now, does it, jackass?"

"All right." Moor continued helping the slave to his feet. The Horseman's flesh was dangerously hot. His bloodshot eyes fixed on Moor's in disbelief. Nodding slightly to the sick Horseman, Moor picked up the harness and put it on.

Across the cave, the big Highlander stared at Moor, his eyes narrowed. After a moment, he continued out of the cave. Probably to the bath. Moor sighed as he leaned into the harness and continued pulling. Washing would feel so damn good right now.

The first slaver curled his lip and started to speak, but the other stopped him and shrugged. "As long as the work gets done. Just make sure our savior here does his fair share."

"What about this one?" the first guard prodded the ill Horseman with his whip.

"Send him back to the slave quarters. If he recovers, fine. If he doesn't, cut up his skinny arse and toss him to the Stonesnakes. "

* * * * *

Moor groaned as he stepped into the slave quarters. His entire body ached, but his legs hurt worst of all. It was an effort just to pick up his hooves and walk from one cave to another. After volunteering to work the shift for the ill slave, his own regular one had followed. Three shifts hauling heavy loads was enough to wear out a full-blooded Highlander, and as Moor painfully remembered, he was *not* a full-blooded Highlander.

Before all four legs gave out entirely, he lowered himself to the ground in a corner of the cave and closed his eyes. The harness had rubbed his man-torso and equine back raw, breaking through the calluses he'd built up over the past weeks. Though tired beyond belief, his skin stung too much for him to sleep.

"You."

Moor opened his eyes and looked up at the enormous Highlander.

"What?" he murmured.

"Come with me."

Moor closed his eyes again. "I'm not moving."

"I said come with me."

"And I said—hey," Moor snarled as the young man hauled him to his feet like he was a child's doll. The son-of-a-bitch must have the strength of ten Horsemen.

Moor followed him out of the cave and down several dark, winding corridors.

"Where are we going?" Moor whispered.

"Quiet, or the guards will hear us."

They turned into a torch-lit cave half-filled with a pool of water.

"Hurry up and wash," the Highlander said.

Moor didn't hesitate. Cool water soothed his flesh. He sighed, closing his eyes as he carefully washed his raw back and man-torso.

"Come on," said the Highlander. "The guards will be coming."

Moor hurried out of the pool and shook himself off, using his hands to wipe water from his face and squeeze out his hair.

Silently, they returned to the slave quarters.

"Thank you," Moor said, settling onto his side. His skin still stung, but the water had cleansed the sores and he felt more refreshed than he had in days.

"Why did you help that slave today?"

"Because someone had to."

"If you care about anybody but yourself, it's like a death sentence in this place."

"You care. That's why you try to keep peace among the slaves. That's even why you encourage them to obey the guards. You think it's the way to make life easiest for them, but it's not."

"You haven't been here as long as I have. I know that to listen and obey is the only way to stay alive."

"You call this living?"

"It's surviving."

Moor stared up at the Highlander. "Don't you want more than that? You're young. You're powerful. If you get out of these mines, you can do so much with your life."

"I'm never getting out of these mines, and neither are you."

Moor stood and beckoned the Highlander to a corner of the cave, far away from the others. "Did you ever think of rallying the slaves and planning an escape?"

The youth's jaw tightened and he glared at Moor. "You must be mad to talk like this."

"This place is enough to drive you mad."

"Listen, I—"

"What's this about?" the gray-coated Horseman approached.

"Nothing," said the Highlander.

"Let me guess, you think you can find a way out of here?" The older man offered Moor a grim smile.

"Has anyone ever tried?"

"Tried? Yes. Succeeded? Never."

"This man is insane," the Highlander continued. "Do you know he took someone else's shift today?"

"Ah. Then it's true." The older Horseman smiled. "We heard that rumor on the upper levels."

"No one does that," the Highlander said.

"At least his actions reflect his words. I respect that."

"Thank you," Moor said. Finally, someone who appreciated a fighting spirit.

"But I'm afraid your good intentions are futile here. Escape is impossible. If the guards don't get you, the Stonesnakes will."

"I can't give up hope."

Susana and Inez must be worried about him, and what about Silas? Every now and then, he heard his nephew was alive and well, but how could he allow him to grow up in captivity? Moor simply could not accept slavery when he—and Silas—had so much to live for outside of the Vertue Mountains.

"If you must cling to hope, then do it," said the gray-coated slave. "Now, I suggest we all get some sleep before our shifts tomorrow."

* * * * *

Two days later, Moor and the Highlander worked together to clear out one of the small caves filled with boulders. With the guards gone for a short time, they were able to talk a bit as they worked. Though the youth was quiet by nature, Moor had learned to appreciate his calmness and underlying determination. The Highlander almost seemed to take pride in his ability to pull heavier loads than any slave and allow no guard to break him, either through overwork or the lash.

"Where did you come from before you were abducted?" Moor asked as they loaded their wagons.

"A village west of here. Mostly Highlanders lived there. It was small, but I liked it."

"Were your parents taken into slavery as well?"

"They were killed."

"I'm sorry."

The Highlander shook his head. "Doesn't matter now. I hardly remember them."

"Then I'm really sorry."

The young man stared at him for a moment. "You are very strange."

Moor smiled. "I'm taking that as a compliment."

They worked in silence for several moments before the Highlander asked, "Did you share dreams with your wife?"

Moor paused, stunned by such a personal question, especially from this young man. "Yes, I did."

"Then it is true. I've heard about dream sharing."

"It's a wonderful thing. If you ever experience it, you'll know why I want to escape from here so badly."

"I hope it never happens to me. Not in this place."

Before the conversation continued, the sound of pounding hooves echoed in the corridor. A scrawny, panting Horseman stuck his head in the cave. "Tam is down."

"What?" the Highlander bellowed, tearing off his harness and charging out of the cave.

Moor ripped off his harness and followed.

"Where?" the Highlander asked the messenger who led the way deeper into the mines.

"Follow me. It's one of the lowest levels."

The three burst into a cave where human slaves chopped at rocks while three Horsemen hauled loads of stones. Their gazes fixed sadly on the Horseman who lay on his side, still harnessed to his wagon, his skin nearly as gray as his dirt-and-sweat matted coat.

The Highlander dropped to his knees beside him, shaking him. "Tam!"

Moor approached, though he knew instantly the gray-coated Horseman was dead. Feeling for a pulse proved him right.

"What the hell was he doing hauling loads down here?" the Highlander roared. "He was too old. He was supposed to be in the upper levels."

"They needed another puller." One of the nearby human slaves glanced over his shoulder. "Poor old bastard. Didn't last an hour in here."

The Highlander's eyes glistened with unshed tears as he removed the harness from his friend.

Two Horseman guards stepped into the cave and approached.

"Shit," one of them said. "I knew we shouldn't bring that old Highlander down here."

"We better chop up his ass and feed it to the Stonesnakes before the carcass stinks up the whole place," said the other. He used the butt of his whip to prod the youth who still held Tam's body. "Drag that carcass outside so we can get chopping."

"You're not touching him," the youth said, his jaw taut.

"What?" roared the guard, lashing the Highlander across the face.

The youth placed Tam aside, but to Moor's surprise, grasped the side of the wagon and, the muscles bulging in his big arms, tipped it over. The rocks inside tumbled over the cave floor and scattered several of the human slaves.

"What are you doing?" bellowed one of the guards as he and his companion pulled back their whips and began beating the youth.

"What *are* you doing?" Moor called.

"Burying him."

Ignoring the blows that lashed his equine back bloody, the Highlander placed Tam's body in the wagon and hitched himself to it. Pushing past the guards, he dragged it out of the cave.

The youth's loyalty and grief touched Moor who followed him.

"Where the hell are you going?" one guard bellowed, turning his whip on Moor as well.

"Forget them," the other slaver snarled. "If they want to bury the stinking carcass, let them. At least it's out of here. The rest of you, get back to work."

Moor followed the wagon up the craggy path to the mine's entrance, picking up two discarded shovels on the way. A short distance from the cave, the Highlander stopped.

"We can't go far," the youth said. "This place is crawling with Stonesnakes."

"All right." Moor gazed around. Completely surrounded by high, barren mountains, Moor sensed the chill in the air wasn't just from the cool weather. There was no vegetation and no animals in sight. Other than the thud of their hooves on the dirt, they were encompassed by eerie silence. He approached the Highlander, his brow furrowing as he noted his bloody back. "We should find some water. A few of those cuts are deep."

"Later." The youth's teeth clenched visibly as he picked up a shovel and dug. "You don't have to help me."

"I don't mind."

It took hours to dig a hole deep enough in the hard, rocky ground to bury Tam's body. Moor glanced at the Highlander several times. He couldn't help feeling for the younger man whose expression revealed his deep caring for the gray-coated Horseman.

It was nearly dark when they finished. The Highlander lowered himself to his knees and stared at the freshly dug grave.

Moor approached and placed a firm hand on his shoulder. "I'm sorry. I know you and he were close."

"I was a child when I first came here. He took care of me, helped me survive. You learn not to care about people here, but I couldn't help being grateful for..." he paused, unable to continue.

"It's all right, son." Moor placed an arm around the other Horseman. It should have seemed strange, a tough old Carrier holding a rugged young Highlander as he cried, but it didn't. Afterward, neither of them mentioned it. Moor hauled a bucket of water from a well near the mine entrance and assisted the Highlander in washing his lashed beast-back. Old scars riddled his skin, obviously the results of severe beatings over the years. In spite of his great size and strength, the Highlander's dark brown coat was almost as soft as a foal's underbelly. Some Horsemen were born with velvet-skinned equine halves. Women seemed to love it, but Moor hated to think about how much more painful rough-treatment felt to a Horseman with that kind of skin.

"I have an idea," Moor said. "Kneel by that rock."

"Why?"

"Just do it."

The Highlander obeyed. Moor approached, placing part of the youth's testicle chain onto a rock and striking it with the shovel.

After several tries, the Highlander stood and said, "I could have told you it wouldn't work. Do you think the rest of us haven't tried? The chains are made of stronger metal than the tools."

Shaking his head, Moor followed the younger Horseman back inside where they accepted the guards' punishment of each of them working an extra shift. It had been worth it. At least one slave had been buried with dignity.

At the end of their extended shift, they retired to the slave quarters.

"My name is Zach," the Highlander said.

Moor nodded. "Glad to finally know you, Zach."

"Tomorrow night, I'll take you to see your nephew."

Moor drew in a sharp breath. "You can do that?"

"It'll be dangerous, but if we're careful, it's possible."

"Thank you."

"Don't thank me yet. If we get caught, it could mean all our lives."

* * * * *

"Uncle Moor." Silas flung his arms around Moor who embraced him tightly. Relief upon seeing his nephew safe washed over him. He'd almost begun to think Silas wasn't at the mine after all.

"Silas, I'm sorry you ended up here. Have you been badly hurt?" Moor held the boy at arm's length. Like the rest of the slaves, he was too thin and scarred from the harness, but he bore no whip marks.

"Not really. As long as I do what I'm told, they don't hit me. Zach's helped me."

Moor glanced at Zach. "I appreciate all you've done." He turned back to Silas. "I'm going to do all I can to find a way out of here."

Moor was glad the boy's eyes widened with hope. At least his spirit hadn't been broken. Yet.

"Why are you giving the boy false hope?" Zach snapped.

"I *am* going to try getting us out of here."

Silas looked at the Highlander. "Don't you want to escape, Zach?"

"It's impossible. I wish I could tell you differently, but I already know." Zach glanced outside the small, dark cave they were crammed into. "We need to go before the guards come."

Moor embraced Silas again and ruffled the boy's hair. "Do what Zach tells you and you'll be all right."

"I will." Silas followed Zach out of the cave, glancing once over his shoulder. "We are going to get out of here, aren't we, Uncle Moor?"

"I will do everything I can to see that we do." Moor wished he could offer a promise instead.

He waited until Zach returned.

"So what is this plan you have for escape?" Zach asked.

"Are you really interested, or are you being sarcastic?"

"A little of both."

"I'm not sure yet. The best I can think of is for most of us slaves to get together and overpower the guards."

"Impossible."

"That we overpower them, or that the slaves rally?"

"They won't rally. They're too afraid."

"You could convince them."

"Me?" Zach's brow furrowed. "Why me?"

"It's obvious that they look to you for leadership."

"I won't do it. If we rebel, slaves will be killed. There's enough violence and death here already."

"Exactly. So if it's our hide to begin with, why don't we get it whipped off trying to benefit ourselves instead of these damn slavers?"

Zach sighed. "I'll think about it."

"All right. It's a start."

"That's all it might be."

In spite of his frustration, Moor refrained from further speech. Zach had spent most of his life in the mine. He'd endured too much for Moor to convince him in a few short weeks that he should help lead a rebellion. Time. In time, he could be convinced. Zach might not even realize it himself but the will, not just to survive but to live, smoldered deep inside him. Moor would do everything in his power to escape, but without Zach's help his plan might never work.

* * * * *

The following morning as Moor made his way to the lower levels, a guard pulled him out of line.

"We need you as a messenger today," he said.

Moor's lip curled. In spite of the heavy loads, he preferred working below. The trails were much easier on the hooves.

He soon realized hooves were the least of his worries. When he reached the upper level, three Horseman slavers approached him. One twisted his testicle chain while another struck him across the face with the flat of his sword. Pain shot through him from head to tail. What the hell were they doing to him now? Moor staggered beneath the blow as the third tossed a rope over his man-torso and pulled tightly, binding his arms to his sides.

"You've been starting trouble with that mouth of yours," growled one of the Horsemen. "You're an animal, but you seem to have forgotten. This will help you remember."

Moor struggled as a thick iron bar was forced into his mouth and fastened in place with a rope tied behind his head. The cold, metallic taste filled his mouth, nearly gagging him. Another rope attached to the iron dangled down his back. The entire contraption mimicked a true-horse's bit and reins.

A human slaver flung a saddle on his back, pulling the girth too tightly. He mounted, the testicle chain in his hand, destroying Moor's urge to fling him off his back.

"Maybe now you'll learn your place," said the guard who'd forced the bit between Moor's lips.

The rider kicked Moor's sides, his spurs almost drawing blood.

The hellish day began.

The slaver rode recklessly, yanking hard on the rope until all Moor tasted was blood from the torn corners of his mouth. He tried moving carefully over the rocky ground, but whenever his pace slowed, the guard twisted the chain and dug his spurred heels into Moor's sides.

If I live through this, I'm going to kill the bastard.

Moor thought to himself as he stood for a moment, catching his breath, while his rider paused to talk with another slaver. Gods, he wished for a drink. Sweat soaked, incredibly thirsty, and weak from pain, he wondered if his life could possibly get any worse.

During the next run, his front hoof split on the rocky path. He stumbled into the cave wall. The rider jerked his chain hard as he almost fell off Moor's back. Nearly blacking out from pain, Moor tried to keep his trembling legs steady. He almost prayed for death, or at least some rest. Where were Susana's gentle hands and soothing kisses when he most needed them?

"Damn it," the rider snarled. To Moor's relief, he dismounted. Glancing at Moor's hoof, he cursed. "Useless. I ain't riding you like that. It's a good way for a man to get killed."

Before Moor could fully recover, the guard tugged on his chain. Exhausted, Moor followed him like a child's pony to a Horseman guard who led him to the lower levels.

"Not so tough now, are you?" the Horseman sneered as he shoved Moor towards a loaded wagon.

Zach and several others glanced at him. The Highlander's mouth opened as if he was about to speak, his eyes reflecting pity and a spark of anger.

"Get to work." The guard's whip fell on Moor's man-back.

Moor stood, unmoving. There was no way he could pull that wagon, not with his hoof in such condition.

Another yank on his chain and Moor took an agonizing step forward, leaning into the harness. Panting, pain shooting up his leg from his injured hoof, he didn't know how he managed to pull the wagon to its destination. The journey back wasn't as bad, but he doubted he could make another. Several human slaves filled the wagon. Halfway out of the cave, Moor's legs gave out. He fell hard. Groaning, he tried to stand. The whip stung his flesh as the guard bellowed at him.

His eyes opened halfway. Someone was removing his harness. Zach dragged him aside and hitched himself to the wagon. The guard had stopped beating Moor and turned his whip on Zach.

Another slaver entered the cave and said, "Looks like now's a good time to test out that new healer. See if she's worth what we're paying her."

"I still say it's a stupid idea having a healer for slaves," said the guard who had stopped beating Zach as the Highlander left the cave, hauling Moor's wagon.

The guards approached just as Moor blacked out.

* * * * *

Susana's stomach churned as she walked around the small cave the slavers had provided for an infirmary. Already the room was nearly filled with severely ill and injured slaves, both human and Horseman. She could hardly believe her plan to enter the mines had worked. It had taken her weeks to find and convince the slavers that it would be more profitable for them to hire a healer to rehabilitate miners instead of allowing them to die, therefore being forced to replace them. The longer the workers lasted, the more profit the slavers made by selling the newly captured ones. They'd finally agreed to test her idea by putting her to work in the mines. She would be paid a fee from their profits. Already she'd labored in two different mines. Finding Moor in neither, she moved on to a third.

She'd hoped for Terra and Inez to join her, but she hadn't waited for them once she'd decided on a plan. All she could cling to was the thought that they would come for her. Once she found Moor she hadn't the slightest idea of how they would escape.

"Here's another one for you," a gruff voice called from the cave entrance. A Horseman who had been assigned to bring her the severely injured workers pulled in a wagon.

Susana's heart momentarily stopped beating as she recognized Moor. Hurrying to the wagon, horror and rage nearly overcame her.

Those bastards had ruined him. His once beautiful coat was a sweat-drenched mass of scars and bloody gashes. Blood smeared his face and oozed from the corners of his mouth plugged with some horrible metal *thing*. Bones stuck out beneath the filthy skin of his underweight frame.

I'm going to kill them.

She pointed to an empty corner. "Put him over there."

Gathering a bucket of water, several clean cloths, salve, and bandages, she knelt beside him, willing her hands to remain steady as she worked.

First the metal and ropes had to go. She untied the rope from behind his head and carefully tugged the metal bar from his mouth, wincing as a fresh flow of blood trickled from his split lips. He moaned, moving his head slightly.

"It's all right," she murmured, gently cleansing his face and lips. Under the watch of the other slaves and random guards popping in and out, she couldn't risk them discovering she was his wife. Leaning close to his ear, she whispered, "It's Susana. I love you so much, my darling."

His eyes opened partway and his gaze fixed on her. His lips formed words that were too soft to hear before he lost consciousness again. For that she was grateful. At least she could scrub his injuries without hurting him more. She finished with the cuts and began feeling his entire body for sprains and broken bones, pausing in disgust at the chains binding his wings to his testicles. When she'd first seen the horrible device used to keep the Horsemen under control, she'd been furious. The metal rings piercing their bodies were welded, so without proper tools, the Horsemen couldn't be freed.

She continued her examination, thinking of ways to steal a metal file or some other piece of equipment from the slavers.

Other than some swelling in his legs, Moor seemed as fit as could be expected of a Horseman who had been starved, beaten, and overworked.

Her anger was renewed when she reached his split hoof. She'd seen so many similar injuries during her time in the mines. The idea of running Horsemen, unshod, over such craggy ground made her furious. She'd tried convincing the slavers to shoe them, but they wouldn't bother with the expense of a blacksmith. Susana had come to believe that was only a half-truth. These slavers enjoyed watching others suffer.

By the time she finished tending Moor, he still hadn't awakened. Covering him with a blanket, she stroked his hair for several moments, scarcely able to believe she'd finally found him. Reluctantly, she left him to sleep while she checked some of her other patients.

Suddenly one of the largest Horsemen she'd ever seen stepped into the cave. As he approached, she noted bloody gashes on his back.

"I'll get some salve for you," she said.

"How is Moor?"

Susana lifted an eyebrow. "He's doing as well as can be expected."

The Horseman nodded. "I almost didn't believe it when they said we have a healer now."

"It took some convincing on my part, believe me."

As Susana cleaned the man's injuries, he watched her over his shoulder, his eyes wary.

"I'll try not to hurt you," she said.

"It doesn't matter."

"You know Moor well?" Curiosity about what had happened to her husband clawed at her.

"He's a good man."

"Yes, he is."

The Horseman raised an eyebrow. "How would you know?"

"I...it just seems that way."

"I see." He stared at her. "So tell me what a healer like you is really doing here?"

Susana drew a sharp breath as her eyes met his. They were large brown eyes. Calm and strong. The expression in them reminded her of Moor's.

"It's all right." He turned away. "I understand secrecy."

"Thank you."

They fell silent as she continued her work.

Though something told her she could trust this Horseman, she couldn't disclose her true identity, not when her life and Moor's hung in the balance.

Chapter Twelve
Plan of Escape

Moor awoke to a soft, gentle hand on his face. A cool cloth tenderly washed the corners of his mouth where the metal and rope had ripped his flesh raw. His tongue felt thick and dry. The taste of old blood made his empty stomach flip over.

He forced his heavy eyelids open, then blinked to clear his vision. His heart pounded against his aching ribs. Susana. No, it couldn't be. He must have been as close to death as he felt. His drifting mind was giving him merciful visions of the woman he loved before he—

"Hello," Susana's hushed voice broke his thoughts. She smiled at him and stroked his forehead, her thumb rubbing soothingly between his eyes.

"Susana?"

She nodded and held a mug of water to his lips. "Try to drink some of this."

It was an effort just to raise his head and swallow, yet the liquid felt so good on his cracked lips and dry throat. As if sensing his struggle, Susana moved behind him, supporting him as he finished the water. He leaned against her, his breathing shallow, every muscle in his body aching. One of his front hooves throbbed and his flesh stung from the lash.

"Do you think you can eat something?"

"Susana, what are you doing here?" His weakness frustrated him.

"Shh," she whispered. "I convinced the slavers to hire me as a healer, telling them it would be more profitable to keep the workers healthy instead of constantly replacing them. I'm going to get you out of here, Moor."

"Are you mad?" He pushed himself to his feet, pain shooting from his injured hoof. His legs trembled so much that he lay down immediately, fearful of collapsing again.

"Will you just stay down?" she snapped.

"It's uncomfortable when I'm in this form."

"I know, but I'm afraid if they see you up they'll send you back to work and you won't make it, Moor."

He sighed. She was right. He doubted he could walk a few feet let alone pull any heavy loads. Overwhelmed by love, gratitude, and pure rage, he stared at her.

"Now that you're here, did you consider how you might get out?"

She shook her head. "I just had to find you. Linn needed approval from that damn General Sota before he could leave. I sent a message to Terra and Inez, but I couldn't just sit there waiting until they got it."

"Gods, Susana, if anything happens to you, I'll never forgive myself." He squeezed her hand, longing to pull her into his arms, but if the slavers realized they were married, he didn't want to consider the consequences.

"It's all right. I have a plan."

"What is it?"

"Hey, you, healer."

Both Moor and Susana turned to the cave entrance through which one of the human slavers strode. Moor's teeth ground. It was the man who'd ridden him with the bit and spurs.

"I need you." The slaver nodded toward his hand wrapped in a bloody cloth.

"Go sit in that alcove." Susana pointed across the cave. "I'll be right with you."

"Bastard," Moor muttered under his breath. "Love to shove a bit in his mouth."

Susana's expression froze as she touched his cracked lips. "He did this to you?"

Moor grasped her wrist. "Forget me. Just do your job and find a way to get out of here."

Susana nodded, her teeth visibly clenched.

"Don't give yourself away," Moor warned.

She forced a smile as she went to tend the slaver.

Leaning against the craggy wall, he stared towards the alcove. Just hours ago, he'd nearly given up, now he had to survive. Susana had risked everything to find him. Surely no man had more to live for than he did. And he couldn't die or rest until he knew she was safely out of the mines.

"Ow. I thought you were a healer, bitch."

Moor pushed himself to his feet, about to charge the alcove, half-dead or not.

"And I thought you were some sort of warrior, not a baby," Susana snapped. "Sit still while I wrap your hand."

Dropping back to the ground, Moor watched as, moments later, Susana stepped back into view, a smirk on her lips. The slaver, his face pale and hand bandaged, hurried out of the cave.

"Whoever said healers have to be gentle, bastard?" she muttered.

A smile tugged at Moor's lips. Gods, he loved her. He noticed several of the other slaves also smiling with gratitude in her direction.

"I'm going to get you some food," she told the group. "I'll be back."

No sooner had she left than Zach appeared in the doorway. He spoke to several of the other slaves before stopping beside Moor.

"How are you feeling?"

"Better. Thank you for finishing my work for me."

"It's nothing you haven't done for others." Zach held Moor's gaze for a long moment.

"What?"

"You know that healer, don't you?"

Fear tightened Moor's chest. If Zach knew, how many others had also noticed? "What makes you say that?"

"Just a feeling. Don't worry. I would never tell anyone."

"I never saw her before today."

"If you say so."

"How's my nephew?"

"Fine."

"I'm sorry you were beaten because of me."

Zach shrugged. "If they don't use the lash for one reason, then it's for another. I have to go. I just wanted to see if you pulled through."

Moor nodded, watching as Zach's massive brown hindquarters left the cave. Sighing, he closed his eyes and drifted into a deep, exhausted sleep.

* * * * *

For the next two days, Moor did little but eat and sleep. With Susana's help, he began healing, though she complained that the horrid living conditions stunted everyone's recovery. The slaves were starving, dirty, and badly overworked. Many, as Moor had been on the day he'd been brought to her, were dehydrated.

Susana managed to get decent food for those in the infirmary. She helped many Horsemen and humans, and most of the slaves took an instant liking to her. This didn't surprise Moor. It had been too long since anyone had shown them a bit of kindness. She'd told him that she'd seen Silas and, other than not being fed enough, the boy was sound.

"I have a plan," Susana whispered to Moor late one night when they sat together in a corner of the infirmary. It would be Moor's last night there. In spite of Susana's protests, the slavers demanded he return to work in the morning. Due to her loving care, he was strong enough to continue in the mines. Already he missed seeing her daily. At least in the infirmary, he could reassure himself that she was safe. If anything should happen to her—he dared not think about it. Escape must be his main focus. "I'm going to tell the guards I want to leave for supplies and to try to recruit other healers, considering the money is so good in the mines. While I'm out, I'll find Terra. I'm sure he's been looking for us. He can convince the Fighting Carriers to take over the mine. They said once they had proof you'd been taken, they'd help."

"Good. I can't wait for you to get out of here."

"I'll be back for you."

"No." He grasped her shoulders.

"Shh," she scolded. "Do you want anyone getting suspicious?"

"Once you're out of here, I want you to stay out." He gripped her arms hard, knowing he must be hurting her a bit, but at that moment all that mattered was ensuring her safety. "Promise me you won't set foot in these mines again."

"All right. I promise."

"Good." He released her.

"Moor, I'm so worried about you." Her hand swept his ribs. "You're not healthy enough to go back to work."

"I'll be fine. Believe me."

"If anything else happens to you, I don't know what I'll do." Tears welled in her eyes. Moor's heart twisted. She was the strongest, most courageous woman he knew. She'd put her life at risk to rescue him from these wretched mines, yet the thought of him being hurt made her weep.

"Don't cry." He brushed moisture from the corners of her eyes. "I'm strong as a…as a horse."

His horrible joke brought the slightest smile to her lips.

"I love you, Susana," he whispered close to her ear. "I'm the luckiest man in the universe to have you as my wife."

"I love you, Moor." She squeezed his hand. "Get some sleep. You'll need it for tomorrow."

He drew a deep breath. That was true enough. Tomorrow, he'd be back in the lower levels, working alongside Zach.

* * * * *

To Moor, the following days were pure torture, not because of the physical punishment, but because he was unable to see Susana. He didn't doubt Zach knew when and how to arrange a visit behind the guards' backs. He trusted Zach, but not enough to risk exposing Susana's true reason for being in the mines.

Days passed, and he wondered how she was, if she'd left yet or if she was still nearby. It shamed him to admit how comforting her presence had been during the first few days when he was almost too injured to move. Just seeing her, hearing her voice, and feeling her touch had meant more to him than he could ever fully express.

One evening, after completing a late shift, Moor unhitched his harness and stretched his sore muscles. Zach approached, rubbing his shoulders and looking as hot and tired as Moor felt.

The Highlander glanced around to ensure they were alone, then whispered, "We're going somewhere tonight."

"Silas?"

"No. Just don't go to sleep right away."

"What's the secret?"

Zach stepped away just as a slaver stuck his head in the cave and growled, "You two move it or else you can work through the night."

Moor followed Zach up the winding path to the slave quarters, his exhaustion forgotten as his mind spun with questions. What was Zach up to?

Other than the sound of snoring and an occasional groan of discomfort, the slave quarters were silent. Moor yawned from sheer weariness as the hours seemed to drip by. Finally Zach approached, nudging him in the arm and motioning for Moor to follow him.

Together, they walked the dark, stony pathways. Zach paused outside a black cave mouth and extended his arm. In spite of his apprehension, Moor stepped inside, picking his footing carefully in the darkness and running his hand along the cave wall for guidance. After making a sharp right turn, dim light flickered at the end of another narrow corridor. His pulse quickening, he stepped inside and drew a sharp breath. Susana gazed at him, her face bathed in the light of a single torch embedded in the wall.

"Moor," she breathed, flinging her arms around him.

He gathered her close, lifting her in his arms and burying his lips in her neck. Gods, she smelled so good and felt even better.

Hearing the thud of hoof beats at the cave's entrance, he placed her down and shoved her behind him.

Zach stepped in, his arms folded across his broad chest. He studied them carefully. "I knew I wasn't wrong about the two of you. Don't worry. I won't tell anyone."

"What are you up to?" Moor demanded.

"I thought you might like some privacy."

"You had no idea that I wouldn't betray your midnight excursions to the slavers," Susana said. "Why would you risk that, Zach?"

"Moor's proven himself trustworthy, and if I was right about you, then you wouldn't be loyal to the slavers."

"What if you were wrong?" Moor shook his head. "I've seen some crazy actions before, but this —"

"Is little different than some of the actions I've seen you take. Other than Tam, you're probably the only person I've ever trusted here." Zach glanced over his shoulder as he turned away. "I'll come for you in half an hour. Any longer than that and you run the risk of being caught."

"Can we trust him?" Susana whispered as the Highlander disappeared.

"I think so." Moor pulled her into his arms, holding her so close he felt her heart beating in time with his. "Gods, I've missed you."

"I'll be leaving in two days, so it shouldn't be much longer before you're freed."

Moor held her at arm's length and gazed deeply into her eyes. "You realize that even if the Fighting Carriers help you, I may not get out of here alive."

"I know."

"Always remember how much I love you."

"As long as you always know how much *I* love *you*."

"Susana," Moor whispered against her lips before claiming them. His hand cupped the back of her head as his tongue tenderly slipped into her mouth and met hers.

Susana looped her arms around his neck as he swept her into her into his arms.

His eyes closed, Moor lost himself in sensation. Gods, he wished he could switch to Huform and make love with her then and there. A new ache flooded his body as one of her hands massaged his chest, her fingers entwining in the matt of hair. She moaned softly, her tongue stroking his. She tasted so warm and sweet. Her small, soft body was such a pleasant weight.

Placing her on the ground, he knelt, his gaze fixed on her. "Mount me."

"But you must be sore from the harness."

"I don't care. I need to feel you on my back. I've missed you so much, Susana. What if this is the last time I ever get to feel you astride me? Don't deny me, my love."

Susana cupped his cheek in her hand and kissed him before slipping onto his back.

Moor sighed with pleasure. Her smooth, bare legs slid over his back and sides. Her hands stroked his withers and shoulders before sliding up his man-back. How many times had he taken her touch for granted? The worst torture he'd endured in these mines had been separation from her.

"Oh, Gods, Moor, I love you so, so much." She slipped her arms around him, gripping his chest and pressing her cheek against his back. Her fingertips traced his ribs. "I could kill every one of them for what they've done to you and these other slaves."

"Don't say that, Susana." He stared at her over his shoulder. "You're the sweetest, kindest woman I've ever known. You save lives, not take them. One day, we'll both be out of here, back in our own home."

"I know we will." She stroked his torso while her knees gripped his sides. "I know it."

Her hands left him momentarily. He groaned when her arms slid around him again and her bare breasts pressed against his man-back. The fleshy globes were so warm and soft, such a marvelous torment. Raising herself with her knees, she rubbed her nipples over his skin while her hands massaged his chest. Moor's pulse raced as desire flooded his entire body. How he longed for fulfillment. In this form, the only way he could experience pure, physical bliss was through her.

"Pleasure yourself," he said in a husky voice.

"I want to so much."

"Use my body, Susana. Let me touch you. I want to feel you come."

Closing his eyes, he lost himself in the softness of her skin and the tender scraping of her spiky nipples against his smooth, human flesh.

"Oh, Moor," she panted, pressing tender kisses to his nape and across his shoulders. Her pelvis brushed the joining of his man-torso and beast-body and he shuddered. Her wet pussy and plump clit rubbing his Turning Point was incredibly arousing. She throbbed and gyrated against him while she licked and kissed his man-back. Moor's pulse sped and his breathing quickened from the unendurable desire flooding his body.

Sliding her arms around him, she caressed his nipples with her fingertips. With a mewl of pleasure, she rocked and rubbed faster, her passion juices seeping into him as she came. She pulsed. Tiny ripples of pleasure traveled from her pussy along his back.

"Gods, ahh," she panted, her fingers gripping his hard chest, her knees tight against his sides.

"Susana, Susana," he murmured, reaching behind him and stroking her ribs and legs. Her heart pounded against his man-back as his own throbbed in his chest.

Moor's front hoof stomped the ground. His head arched back and his breathing hoarsened as if he'd just hauled a full load uphill.

Susana sank onto him, her arms resting languidly on his ribs, her lips against his back. "I love you, Moor. I love you so much."

"I love you, too." A ripple of unfulfilled need traveled up his spine. Gods, how he adored her. He prayed for the day when they would be free again and these dreaded mines a fading memory.

* * * * *

The night Zach had arranged was the last time Susana saw Moor before leaving the mines. She'd convinced the slavers that she needed supplies from one of the villages and also planned to recruit another healer. Her heart pounded as the Horseman slaver assigned to fly her out of the Vertue Mountains sped through the sky. He wasn't a smooth flier like Moor and she clung to the harness just to avoid falling to her death.

By the time they landed, all her old fear of flying had nearly returned, but she thought of Moor and how wonderful it felt astride him and her apprehension diminished.

"I'm borrowing a true-horse in the village," she told the slaver.

He narrowed his piercing blue eyes. "Why?"

"Because some of the people I deal with for supplies have an aversion to Horsemen. You could make my trading relationships difficult. I'll meet you back in this spot in three days."

"That's a long time," the slaver grumbled.

"It's what I need. Besides, don't you want some time away from that stinking mine?" Susana flicked her thumb in the direction of the brothel in the center of town. Several of the whores, half-dressed and their dyed hair flowing, cast lustful looks at the slaver.

He shrugged, lifting his wings and drawing a breath that expanded his broad, dark-skinned chest. "I suppose I can occupy my time. If you're not here in three days, I'm leaving and you can find your own way back to the mines."

Susana nodded. She turned and disappeared in the crowd, searching for the livery stable where she might borrow a horse. She needed to ride to the next village that hosted Gatherings. There she could perhaps find a Horseman willing to fly her north to the Hall of Fighting Carriers. She wished she could locate Terra or Linn first, but that might be impossible, considering they were probably out looking for her and Moor.

As Susana reached the stable, an exquisite black stallion being groomed by an equally exquisite black-haired woman caught her attention.

"Phillipa," Susana shouted. Several horses started at the sharpness of her tone, including the stallion who half-reared.

"Easy, Black Silk. Easy, boy." Phillipa, Terra's sister, quickly brought him to his feet. She turned to Susana and dragged her into a crushing embrace.

"Gods, Susana. Where the hell have you been? Do you have any idea how long we've been looking for you? Inez is beside herself. Terra and Linn have been flying all over creation and—"

"Phillipa, I've found Moor and Silas," Susana interrupted, grasping the woman's forearms. "I need to get to Terra and Linn fast."

"Inez is staying at the inn two villages away. She's waiting for Terra. He's been searching the Vertue Mountains for weeks. Linn's been questioning slavers in the tropics. Where are Moor and Silas?"

"At a mine in the Vertue Mountains. It's very well-hidden, but I can bring Terra there. We'll need the Fighting Carriers with us, if they'll come," Susana said bitterly.

"They'll come. You know how much influence Terra has with General Sota."

Phillipa brought Black Silk to his stall, then guided Susana to the inn.

"Susana?" Inez's eyes widened when the two women stepped into the room. Inez embraced Susana tightly with one arm since Canyon was snug in her other. The plump boy squirmed when Susana hugged him. Inez placed the child on the floor at her feet while she and Phillipa listened to Susana's story.

By the time Terra returned at dusk, all three women were furious enough to charge the mine themselves. Terra listened, his ears pinned and eyes blazing with rage, yet when he spoke it was with the calculating calmness that made him such a coveted Fighting Carrier.

"Phillipa, send a message to Linn in the tropics. I'm flying to the Hall of Fighting Carriers right now."

"Will they help?" Susana asked. "They don't think much of Moor because of how he left them so many years ago."

"They'd better help, or else they'll lose me for certain. The Fighting Carriers were formed to protect others against bastards like the slavers. They might just need to be reminded of that."

Chapter Thirteen
The Rebellion

Curses soared through Moor's mind as he leaned into the harness and pulled. Since talking with Susana, he'd formulated his own plan for a possible escape. He needed to convince Zach to talk to the other slaves about rebelling. If they banded together, Moor knew they could take the mine and free themselves, but fear controlled them as much as chains and the lash. Perhaps more.

Moor glanced up as he hauled his load toward the cave entrance. He momentarily forgot to breathe.

Susana's gaze riveted to his before she approached the slave nearest her. What the hell was she doing? The only comfort he had of late was knowing she'd finally left the mines. Now she'd broken her promise and returned. In spite of his anger, hope sparked inside him. If she was back, then she must have reached Terra and Linn. She stopped by each slave and tended their injuries. Moor carried out two loads before she finally approached him.

"I told you not to come back here," he whispered as she applied salve where the harness had rubbed his flesh raw. The strong smelling ointment stung a bit, but at least it would prevent infection.

"I had to. Do you think Zach can arrange a meeting for us? Linn is here with me. He's posing as another healer. He and Terra have a plan, but we'll need the slaves' help."

Moor snorted. "Try and get it. These people are too afraid to fight for themselves."

"You said they'd listen to Zach."

"He's as stubborn as the rest of them, except I don't think he's afraid for himself. He takes too many risks with his own life. He wants to protect the others and thinks avoiding confrontation is the way to do it."

"Do you think he'll meet with us?"

Moor glanced in the direction of the Highlander who looked at them from the corner of his eye. "Yes. I think he will."

"Make it as soon as possible."

"I will."

"I love you," she murmured.

Moor held her gaze, whispering in a voice raw with emotion, "I love you more than anything. Why did you come back here?"

"Trust me." She ran a gentle hand across his equine shoulder. "Just trust me."

* * * * *

"I can't believe you people." Zach's hands balled into fists as his gaze swept Moor, Susana, and Linn.

The four crammed into a small, mid-level cave, dark except for the candle Susana held. Its light flickered against her face, accentuating her pert nose and glistening eyes. Moor's heart swelled with love for her. Never had anyone sacrificed so much for his sake. If he survived, he planned to spend the rest of his life fulfilling her needs and desires.

"Zach, this is our only chance to get out of here," Moor said. "It's the one way to free everybody."

"Not everybody. Some of us will die."

"You're dying anyway," Linn observed. The young, blond Fighting Carrier's expression revealed his annoyance at Zach's resistance to their plan. "I've been here a few short days and already I want to fight the bastards. How can you not want to destroy them after all these years in the mines?"

"You're not a slave like the rest of us. You can leave here whenever you want." Zach lifted his wings just enough to rattle his testicle chain. "Try wearing one of these and see how much you want to fight. You don't know what they do to slaves who try to escape. I do."

"I know you're not afraid for yourself, Zach," Moor said quietly. "I've seen the rebellion in you. What is it that stops you from taking the freedom you deserve and helping the rest of us do the same?"

Zach drew a deep breath, his muscular chest expanding. "We're not made to kill."

"Oh, please." Linn raised his eyes to heaven. "You're worried about killing these sons-of-bitches who've made your life hell?"

"They can ruin my life, but not my spirit."

"Zach," Susana rested a hand on his arm, "I know you care about the other slaves. If you really believe the rebellion will fail, even with the help of the Fighting Carriers, then you can't do it."

"Susana," Linn snapped.

Moor held up his hand and stared into Zach's eyes as he continued where his wife left off, "But if you think there's even a chance that we can take the mine and put an end to the suffering, do you really want to let that chance pass?"

Zach turned, running both hands through his hair. "Gods. Even if I want to do it, I can't guarantee the others will."

"They'll listen to you," Moor pressed. "You know it."

"I'm leaving in the morning," Linn said. "The Fighting Carriers will arrive in two days. You know our plan. We'll attack from the outside while you slaves fight from the inside. If you do what we ask, we will take the mines. The Fighting Carriers will not give up until it's ours. Convince your companions to do their part, Zach. It is your only chance."

The young Fighting Carrier brushed past the others as he left the cave.

Moor took Susana's hand and squeezed it. All his senses screamed danger, yet their plan was their only chance to escape the tortures of the Vertue Mountains. It was his risk to take, but not Susana's. "You're going with Linn."

"No. We've already discussed it. Linn will inform Terra and the others that we've told you our plan. If we both go, it will rouse suspicion among the slavers. They might follow us. Linn hasn't been here long. He can say he doesn't like the working conditions and is leaving."

Moor's jaw tightened. Fear for Susana's safety clawed his gut. Still, her words made sense and he knew she wouldn't leave now that her mind was made up. Had he been free, he would have forced her to go.

"I only wish there was some way to free all of you from these chains," Susana said. "The guards even check our healing supplies before allowing us in the mines. We couldn't smuggle in any files and they won't let us near things like axes."

"We'll fight anyway," Moor said. "As long as Zach agrees to convince the others."

* * * * *

Moor glanced around the cave as he helped two human slaves fill his wagon with rocks. Though everyone appeared outwardly calm, tension hung in the air. Today the Fighting Carriers would come. Today the slaves would either fight for their freedom or forfeit their chance to live without bonds.

Once their plan was disclosed, word traveled fast throughout the mine. In spite of their fear and initial protest, most of the slaves had agreed to follow Zach. If the big Highlander fought, they would back him.

Moor turned his gaze to Zach, who had just returned from his last haul. The young man had been quieter than usual that morning. Though Moor felt in his heart Zach would fight, part of him remained uncertain.

Suddenly shouting erupted from the corridor. Several Horseman slavers galloped past the cave mouth heading upward.

Moor's pulse raced. It had begun. His gaze met Zach's. The two unhitched themselves from their wagons. The other slaves tensed, but followed the two Horsemen of the cave and onto the rebellion.

They had only traveled a short way when hoards of slaves nearly stampeded them as they pushed into the lower level. Shouting and cracking whips echoed above shouts of fear and pain. Chains rattled and several of the humans and Horsemen fell beneath scrambling feet and hooves.

Moor's teeth clenched with rage as he pulled a woman off the rocky ground. Her face and chest were doused in blood.

"What the hell are you doing?" Moor bellowed at the cringing slaves. "Fight them."

"Get down there, you sacks of horseshit," roared one of the slavers, yanking hard on two of the Horsemen's testicle chains. It seemed as if all of the guards had banded together as a weapon-wielding barrier, pushing the slaves backward. Moor knew the Fighting Carriers must have already breached the mine's upper levels.

Above the frantic sounds, metal clinked against rock.

"They're trying to seal us in," shouted one of the slaves from the front. Bits of rock tumbled onto their heads.

Gods, it was true. Moor's breathing quickened with terror. The slavers were hammering the overhanging rocks in an effort to trap them in the lower levels.

Moor dropped the corpse he carried and forced his way forward. "Push ahead. Fight them!" The sting of the lash struck him full in the chest as he neared the slavers. As he yanked the whip from a guard's hand, an arrow embedded in his shoulder. Pain flared through his torso. He staggered but continued fighting.

Suddenly, Zach burst through the crowd. His massive body plunged into the slavers, clearing a space for the miners. One of the Horseman slavers managed to grasp Zach's testicle chain and pulled. Others surrounded him with whips and spears. As Moor rushed to help his friend, Zach did the unspeakable. Grasping his own chains, he bellowed in pain as he tore them from his flesh. The big Highlander was free. Slavers ran, but each of his massive hands lashed out, grasping two slavers by their necks. The snap of breaking bones echoed through the cave.

"Get out of here. Fight," Zach roared at the terrified slaves as he flung the dead guards aside.

For the first time their hollow expressions burned with hope. To Moor's relief, they fought.

Moor grasped a spear from the hands of a nearby guard before the man rammed it through his chest. He kicked and stabbed, clearing another path that the slaves poured through.

"Lead them out," Zach shouted to Moor. The Highlander charged again, keeping the attention of most of the slavers who sought to restrain him.

"This way," Moor bellowed. "Keep fighting."

Ignoring the pain in his lacerated body, Moor plowed through waves of slavers. Zach had been right. There were more than he thought. As they neared the upper levels, a group of Fighting Carriers joined them.

Within moments, the slavers were killed or held captive by the elite Horseman Warriors.

"Moor," Terra shouted.

"Terra." Moor cantered toward his friend. "Where's Susana and Silas?"

"Silas is outside. He's fine. I haven't seen Susana."

"Gods." Moor gritted his teeth as he turned back down the corridor to find his wife, with Terra at his heels. "Go help Zach below. He was surrounded. If not for him, we all might have died."

"Zach?"

"Huge. Highlander. You won't miss him."

Terra nodded and motioned for a small group of Fighting Carriers to follow him deeper into the mine.

Moor galloped down the winding corridors, leaping over bodies of dead and wounded miners and slavers, not caring that the sharp rocks cut his hooves. Susana. If anything had happened to her, he'd never forgive himself.

"Moor."

He stopped suddenly and spun, panting. Susana peered at him from where she'd wedged herself in a tiny space in the rocks, close to the ceiling.

Moor reached up as she squeezed out of the space. She clung to him as he held her close. She was alive. Closing his eyes, he buried his face in her hair and thanked the Gods.

"Oh, Moor," she whispered, her face pressed against his neck. "I thought you might be dead."

"I though the same about you. I love you so much, Susana." He lowered her to the ground. "We need to get back to the upper level. The Fighting Carriers have control there and I'm sure within moments they'll have the whole mine."

"You're hurt." Her hands slid over his bloody chest, the arrow still protruding from his shoulder.

"I'll be fine." He took her hand as they made their way to the upper level. Halfway there, they met Terra and Zach.

Covered in blood and sweat, the Highlander wore a grim expression.

"I thought they got you for sure." Moor rested a firm hand on Zach's shoulder. The Highlander shook his head, his brow furrowed. "Are you all right?"

Zach didn't reply but moved ahead of the others, his gait a bit awkward from ripping away his testicle chains. Moor winced. The young man had courage, that was for certain.

"When we found him, he'd killed a cave full of slavers," Terra said. "If the Fighting Carriers took Highlanders, I'd recruit him for sure."

Moor's gaze followed Zach. "Somehow I don't think he'd want to make a living out of fighting, anyway."

"The mine is almost all clear. Come topside so you can get cleaned up and those injuries tended. And Moor, it's good to see you." Terra clasped the older Horseman's uninjured shoulder. "Inez has been beside herself."

"Thank you for what you've done, Terra. You and Linn." Moor touched Susana's cheek and gazed at her with all the love he felt. "And I owe you my life, my beautiful Susana."

She smiled slightly and took his hand. "You are the most important thing in my life, Moor. I'll do anything for you."

"I thank the Gods for you, my love." He bent to kiss her.

Susana's hands tenderly stroked his face as her tongue met his.

Terra cleared his throat. "I'll meet you up there."

Moor and Susana hesitantly broke apart. Hand in hand they followed the Fighting Carrier to freedom.

Epilogue
Two Weeks Later

"That tickles." Susana giggled, curling her toes in the grass and tightening her fingers in Moor's hair as he licked the joining of her thighs to her pelvis.

"Mmm," he groaned, moving his head slightly to lick her clit. His hands slid beneath her, his callused palms cupping her rump and raising her closer to his mouth.

"Ah," she cried when the tip of his tongue rolled over the very top of her clit. Nothing felt as good as rolling around on a sunlit field with this man she loved so much. She squirmed as his lips tugged at her sensitive little nubbin.

Susana's heart raced. She crossed her legs behind his neck, clinging so tightly she would have choked a human male. A nice, strong Horseman neck was perfect for clutching when the most wonderful orgasm waited just around the corner...

"Moor," she scolded, writhing with unfulfilled desire as he pulled away. She needn't have worried. His powerful body covered hers, his muscles as hard as the cock that plunged deep inside her, stirring her. "Oh, Gods. Yes. Yes. Yeesss."

He thrust long and fast. Shudders rippled down her spine as she erupted in a climax that seemed to turn her to liquid. Smiling, she reflected that making love was exactly like flying. Thrilling. Wild. A timeless ecstasy.

As the marvelous throbbing pleasure ebbed, her limbs relaxed, falling to the sun-warmed grass. Moor lowered himself as well, supporting most of his weight on his forearms.

"I love you, Susana," he purred against her lips.

"I'm going to miss you this afternoon."

"Terra and I won't be gone long. We'll meet Zach and bring him to Hornview."

"I'm glad he decided to move here. I hated leaving him in those horrible ruins."

"It was his home once, before the slavers destroyed it. I understand why he wanted to spend some time alone there."

"I only wish our home hadn't been ruined during that lightning storm while we were in the mines," Susana sighed. "All that work you did building the herbarium for me—not to mention the cottage itself—is ruined."

"I'll build another one."

"Almost all your beautiful books were destroyed."

"They were things, Susana. We enjoyed them, but they can be replaced. What I care about is you, Inez, Canyon, and our friends."

"You're right." She gazed at him and traced his lips with her fingertip. "When you get back, we can work more on having our own baby."

"Why wait?" He smiled, a lustful expression in his eyes that sent her heart pounding. He shifted his hips, his still-hard cock rubbing her soft, wet pussy. "Give me something to remember on my flight."

Susana grinned, slipping her arms around his neck and covering his mouth with hers. With Moor, the perfect day seemed even more perfect, the soft grass beneath her even softer. Suddenly she felt as if life had just begun again. They were together, free, and so very much in love.

The End

About the author:

A lifelong fan of action and romance, Kate Hill likes heroes with a touch of something wicked and wild. Her short fiction and poetry have appeared in publications both on and off the Internet. When she's not working on her books, Kate enjoys dancing, martial arts, and researching vampires and Viking history.

Kate welcomes mail from readers. You can write to her c/o Ellora's Cave Publishing at 1056 Home Ave. Akron, Oh 44310-3502.

Why an electronic book?

We live in the Information Age—an exciting time in the history of human civilization in which technology rules supreme and continues to progress in leaps and bounds every minute of every hour of every day. For a multitude of reasons, more and more avid literary fans are opting to purchase e-books instead of paperbacks. The question to those not yet initiated to the world of electronic reading is simply: *why?*

1. *Price.* An electronic title at Ellora's Cave Publishing and Cerridwen Press runs anywhere from 40-75% less than the cover price of the <u>exact same title</u> in paperback format. Why? Cold mathematics. It is less expensive to publish an e-book than it is to publish a paperback, so the savings are passed along to the consumer.

2. *Space.* Running out of room to house your paperback books? That is one worry you will never have with electronic novels. For a low one-time cost, you can purchase a handheld computer designed specifically for e-reading purposes. Many e-readers are larger than the average handheld, giving you plenty of screen room. Better yet, hundreds of titles can be stored within your new library—a single microchip. (Please note that Ellora's Cave and Cerridwen Press does not endorse any specific brands. You can check our website at www.ellorascave.com or

www.cerridwenpress.com for customer recommendations we make available to new consumers.)

3. *Mobility*. Because your new library now consists of only a microchip, your entire cache of books can be taken with you wherever you go.

4. *Personal preferences are accounted for*. Are the words you are currently reading too small? Too large? Too...**ANNOYING**? Paperback books cannot be modified according to personal preferences, but e-books can.

5. *Instant gratification*. Is it the middle of the night and all the bookstores are closed? Are you tired of waiting days—sometimes weeks—for online and offline bookstores to ship the novels you bought? Ellora's Cave Publishing sells instantaneous downloads 24 hours a day, 7 days a week, 365 days a year. Our e-book delivery system is 100% automated, meaning your order is filled as soon as you pay for it.

Those are a few of the top reasons why electronic novels are displacing paperbacks for many an avid reader. As always, Ellora's Cave and Cerridwen Press welcomes your questions and comments. We invite you to email us at service@ellorascave.com, service@cerridwenpress.com or write to us directly at: 1056 Home Ave. Akron OH 44310-3502.

COMING TO A BOOKSTORE NEAR YOU!

ELLORA'S CAVE
2005
BEST SELLING AUTHORS TOUR

Discover for yourself why readers can't get enough of the multiple award-winning publisher Ellora's Cave. Whether you prefer e-books or paperbacks, be sure to visit EC on the web at www.ellorascave.com for an erotic reading experience that will leave you breathless.

www.ellorascave.com